THE ORANGE SPONG

AND

STORYTELLING AT THE VAMP-ART CAFÉ

ST SUKIE DE LA CROIX

RATTLING GOOD YARNS
PRESS
PALM SPRINGS, CALIFORNIA

Rattling Good Yarns Press
33490 Date Palm Drive 3065
Cathedral City CA 92235
USA
www.rattlinggoodyarns.com

Cover Design: Ian Henzel
Divider graphic courtesy of AmethystManiac
Library of Congress Control Number: 2020937676
ISBN: 978-1-7341464-4-8

For Lucy Anna Marie, my daughter

CONTENTS

ONE

AN EVENING OF STORYTELLING BEGINS

Ra, the orange spong, sank over the Chicago rooftops and the manager of the Vamp-Art Café unlocked the door, pushed it open. He then hung a WELCOME sign in the window next to a tattered menu – curling, brown-edged, lettering faded, from years of the blistering late-morning sun on this, the west side of the street. He was an elderly man with a wrinkled, gnarly face. His face resembled a street map of Carthage after the ravages of the third Punic War – a war he fought in, alongside the Carthaginians, against the might of the Roman Empire. The manager teetered unsteadily, gripping tightly onto the silver Bastet head of his walnut walking cane. His knuckles were deathly white. Depending on the light, he resembled a fresh corpse, perhaps two days old. However, instead of smelling of rotten fruit and bad eggs, the manager of the Vamp-Art Café was known for wearing Fougère Royale, a fragrance created by his friend, Jean-François Houbigant, in 1882. The manager of the Vamp-Art Cafe was certainly not dead. Neither was he alive.

The manager's name was Oliver Cramfish. He had been the lover of James I of Britain, William Shakespeare, and Ann Boleyn, though not at the same time or in the same bed. Cramfish also shared a brief, but passionate, liaison with Joan of Arc. That was before she was la Pucelle d'Orléans and canonized by Pope Benedict XV. Before her visions of Archangel Michael, St. Margaret, and St. Catherine of Alexandria. Before she was tied to a pillar at the Vieux-Marché in Rouen and burned alive, a "supposed" virgin. Cramfish knew her when she was plain Jeanne d'Arc, daughter of peasants Jacques d'Arc and Isabelle Romée, in Domrémy in North-East France.

Like all vampires, Oliver Cramfish had stories to tell.

Three wait staff, two girly-boys, and one boyish-girl stood behind the counter, backs stiff in their black uniforms, and starched white aprons. Their freshly brushed fangs bared and gleaming. It was a challenge telling them apart. Boys wearing rouge, powder, and lipstick, were commonplace in this neighborhood. You couldn't walk down the street without tripping over a sissy or two. Some of these hubristic girly-boys were vampires, others not. Some were Roman Catholic. Some were poets. Some were both. Some were Sapphic or Uranian. Others were none of the above. Others were all of the above. Boyish-girls smoking cigars and strutting the streets swinging silver-top canes, wearing men's suits and a monocle, were also a common sight in this neighborhood. These women wore homburg hats with dented crowns and stiff brims shaped like kettle-curls.

On the subject of vampire fangs, a regular toothpaste advert in the *Chicago Tribune* read:

"Be the one to outwit pyorrhea – using Forham's toothpaste twice a day."

Most vampires used Forham's, or to be accurate, vampires who care about personal hygiene used it. As the advert proclaimed, it was "simply the best." Of course, not all vampires are human, some are vegetables, others are pieces of furniture. A carrot can be a vampire, or a sofa bed, or a wall, or a whale. It's a little-known fact that vampirism is nothing more, nor less, than global acupuncture. Vampire fangs are needles that pierce the "afflicted" to drain away the deadly poison known as "the fear of death."

Confused? We will talk more of this later.

Oliver Cramfish tutored his staff with precision, not unlike maestro Gustav Mahler conducting the New York Philharmonic Orchestra in Richard Wagner's *Tristan and Isolde*. Cramfish threw back his head, turkey wattle dangling, and shrieked orders into the ether. "You will use Hennafoam shampoo, Delica Kiss-proof lipstick and Shinola polish on your shoes!" This was no request but a dictate, and nobody argues with a 4,000-years-old vampire who performed cunnilingus on Joan of Arc. You just didn't do that.

It's 1924, and the Vamp-Art Café in Chicago's Towertown opens from 6 p.m. 'til midnight, seven days a week. The neighborhood is inhabited by bohemians, burlesque and vaudeville stars, film actors, writers, artists, poets, political radicals, circus and fairground folk, female and male impersonators, hobos, "temperamentals," and vampires.

Many of the denizens of this cesspool of infamy were movie extras and failed stars left behind from the Essanay film studios, a jewel in Chicago's crown before it upped and moved to Hollywood. Essanay made stars of George Periolat, Ben Turpin, Wallace Beery, Thomas Meighan, Colleen Moore, Francis X. Bushman, Gloria Swanson, Ann Little, Helen Dunbar, Lester Cuneo, Florence Oberle, Lewis Stone, Virginia Valli, Edward Arnold, Edmund Cobb, and Rod La Rocque. Mostly now forgotten, dying stars, in the dark and distant galaxy of the past. The weather in Chicago was not suited to on-location filmmaking, unless you needed a snow scene. How many versions of *A Christmas Carol* can you make? How many do you need? It was also impossible to produce the increasingly popular cowboy movies in the Windy City, like Buster Keaton's *The Paleface* or Hoot Gibson's *The Bear Cat*. The only sand in Chicago lay on the beaches of Lake Michigan, and the only canyons lay between skyscrapers on State Street. Chicago's loss was Hollywood's gain. However, the arts were not dead in Chicago. The city still had Towertown. Twelve square blocks of garish color in a black and white city of big shoulders, prohibition, illegal hooch and hoodlums.

The Vamp-Art Café was located on North Clark Street between the Goldstein furniture store and Maurice L. Rothschild's, a men's clothing emporium specializing in George A. Mabbett & Sons worsted tweed suits. It was also near Bughouse Square. A free-speech forum where radicals, poets, religionists, and assorted crackpots, spoke passionately on subjects ranging from anarchism to the invasion of Earth by blob-fish from outer space. One regular, a woman wearing cocaine-spoon earrings, claimed she was a Dadaist, stood on a soapbox, and repeated Da-Da-Da-Da-Da-Da-Da until she was hoarse.

Although open to everyone, only vampires frequented the Vamp-Art Café, because only the undead could find it. Non-vampires walked past it in a trance as if it wasn't there. Not even the ceramic fangs dangling over the door caught their attention, or the vials of rhesus negative blood in the window – not that vampires drink blood because they don't. The window display – created by Cramfish – was "ironic" and the cause of much amusement amongst Chicago's undead. By placing fangs and blood in the window, they reclaimed the stereotype of vampires as blood-sucking monsters. Sometimes, Cramfish hung garlic, a silver bullet, and a crucifix in the window.

Inside the café was a counter, a small stage, and twelve tables, four chairs at each, with white tablecloths, blue napkins, gold napkin rings, and purple glass salt-and-pepper shakers. Above the countertop, a sign read:

Anyone or any "thing" can live forever.

Since the Puritans landed at Plymouth Rock in 1620, America has welcomed "undesirables" from over the various borders and ponds. Chicago, being politically corrupt and bereft of morals, is a magnet for Europe's detritus – a city of ne'er-do-wells, fraudsters, gangsters, whores, and con artists. Those shunned elsewhere are welcomed in the Windy City with open arms, open wallets, and open legs.

At the base of New York's Statue of Liberty, the Emma Lazarus poem reads:

Give me your tired, your poor,
Your huddled masses yearning to breathe free,
The wretched refuse of your teeming shore.
Send these, the homeless, tempest-tossed, to me:
I lift my lamp beside the golden door.

Indeed, waves of wretched refuse did wash-up on America's shore. The Irish fled the Emerald Isle to escape the potato famine. Jews escaped marauding Cossacks and Russian pogroms. Italian anarchists escaped persecution. The Dutch fled the horror of wearing clogs and growing tulips. And, vampires escaped the publication of Bram Stoker's book, *Dracula*. In 1897, Archibald Constable and Co. published *Dracula* by the Irish author Bram Stoker, a book portraying vampires in an unsympathetic light, to say the least. Fearing backlash and pogroms, British vampires packed their bags. They fled to America, landing at the sweaty buzzing beehive of Ellis Island. Unlike the Jews and Irish escaping oppressive governments, vampires fled from the publication of a book. Sadly, *Dracula* followed them across the Atlantic two years later, published by Doubleday & McClure in New York. You can run from Cossacks, you can run from rotting potatoes, you can even run from tulips and clogs, but you can't run away from a book. Books have legs, strong legs with muscular thighs. Books are Olympian track-runners. Books can outrun Spartacus or any other Thracian gladiator in the Roman Empire. Books will hunt you down and drive a stake through your heart.

The menu at the Vamp-Art Café listed no blood brownies or Bloody Marys, just regular offerings and, from under-the-counter, the fruit of the juniper tree in violation of the Volstead Act. Vampires love gin. It makes them maudlin. It makes them cry. It makes them tell stories and respond to stories told to them. Items on the supper menu at the Vamp-Art Café include Brook trout, Amandine; Scotch woodcock; spaghetti, Tetrazzini; Breast of Philadelphia chicken; chilled tomato stuffed with chicken salad. Desserts were baked Alaska; cream puff, Chantilly; ladyfingers; and Coupe St. Jacques.

Not all Chicago's vampires frequented the Vamp-Art Café but those who did were there to celebrate vampire culture. This is where songs were sung and stories told – campfire stories, folk tales, handed down from one generation of vampires to the next. There's nothing vampires like more than a rattling good yarn and the Vamp-Art Café is where the yarns of the undead rattled like rutting skeletons in a tin box.

Tonight, the café was crowded. Popular poet, Dario Brone, was Master of Ceremonies. Brone was 430 years of age, a mass of black curly hair piled atop his head. It looked like a giant tarantula dropped from the ceiling and was busily devouring his skull. Dapper, he wore a pinstripe jacket, white bucks, spats, a bow tie, a vest, and Oxford bags. His cheeks slightly rouged, pink lipstick applied in a "Cupid's Bow" on the upper lip, and the lower lip exaggerated slightly. Brone, head bowed, pressed his fingertips together and held them to his lips as if praying. He closed his eyes. It helped him focus. He breathed deeply, in through his nose, out through his mouth.

Brone was born in Békéscsaba in Crişana, between Romania and Hungary. An orphan, his parents died in a flood when the river Körös burst its banks and flooded their timber-framed house. A twelve-year-old Dario Brone clung to a door while rushing water buffeted the young boy downstream. Two days later he washed up on the riverbank near the estate of vampire Kristóf Török who sheltered the boy, dealt him the Judgment card from the Visconti di Modrone tarot pack and rebirthed him as a vampire. Brone later moved to London.

Brone stepped onto the small stage. The audience fell silent. "We are here to keep our vampire history and culture alive. Tonight, we celebrate the ancient vampire tradition of sharing our favorite stories. These are true vampire tales, told by vampires, for vampires, unlike Bram Stoker's *Dracula*. The assembled vampires booed, hissed, and bared their fangs. "That terrible libelous book is why we sit here in exile. As we all know, that book was published in 1897, the same year the offices of London publisher Archibald Constable and Company burnt down. Do you think that was a coincidence?" The customers at the Vamp-Art Café laughed. All of them knew the arsonist, though her name was never spoken out loud. Brone stiffened. "But let's not weigh down the evening by discussing that book. Let's move on."

"It wasn't only that book that libeled us. Two years ago, there was a film made. Has anyone else seen it? F.W. Furnau's *Nosferatu, eine Symphonie des Grauens*. Giorgio Graffelley, a vampire with greasy hair and a slight lisp, sipped his tea. "I've seen it."

Brone bristled. "I've seen it too, and it's an abomination of German Expressionism. But I've heard that Stoker's wife, Florence, sued the filmmaker and a court ruling dictated that all copies of the film be destroyed."

"Not true." Graffelley shot back. "Yes, they were supposed to destroy all copies but some survived. If both you and I have seen the film, then others must have too. I fear the damage has already been done. Both the book and the film have misrepresented us. We don't all drink blood and sleep in coffins. In fact, to my knowledge, none of us drink blood or sleep in coffins."

The assembled vampires laughed at the absurdity.

Lumia, a Spanish hermaphrodite vampire, stood up. "I haven't read the book or seen the film, but aren't we supposed to turn into bats? That's what somebody told me. All vampires turn into bats. And we are weakened by sunlight."

"In *Nosferatu, eine Symphonie des Grauens,* the vampire is killed by sunlight." Graffelley stifled a giggle.

Lumia shuffled uncomfortably in her seat. "I also heard that vampires can be killed by a stake driven through the heart and that we are frightened of crucifixes and garlic."

The room erupted into guffaws.

"I love garlic." Graffelley called to a waiter. "Garçon, bring me more garlic please."

"Stoker wasn't entirely wrong because some of us can turn into bats." Lilith Korda, a tall thin vampire with a blond bob and an ostrich-feather fan dangling from her wrist, crumbled into dust, out of which flew a bat. Korda circled the café and hung upside-down from the cornice.

Lumia clutched her pearls, astonished. "How do you do that? I can't do that."

"Vampires are not all the same." Graffelley sat up, warming to the subject. "As we all know, vampires are not always human either. There are vampire vegetables, dolls house furniture, steam robots, cutlery, and many other objects. A vampire is nothing more than something or someone who is gifted with everlasting life. That's the beginning and end of it. Vampirism is not about blood, or coffins, or feeding on virgins, it's about living forever. It's about life, not death. Eternal life."

The other vampires applauded. Brone waited for the applause to die down. "Listen my friends, we will waste no more time on that book and film, both created by mortals weighed down and tainted with their own fear of death. Let us leave them to rot in their own misery. Tonight, we are gathered in the Vamp-Art Café to hear vampire stories, immortal tales told by and for immortals. Our first vampire story tonight will be told by Edwin Karayan."

A short, stocky vampire, Karayan sported a bushy soup-strainer mustache, cheery countenance, and plump, rosy red cheeks – an ideal subject for a Dutch master to paint. He wore a white peasant shirt, cracked brown leather shoes, and ill-fitting pants held up by a thick leather belt. He was an armchair futurist, an avid reader of H.G. Wells and Jules Verne. A blacksmith by trade, he was born in Vagharshapat, Armenia, but had spent the last few years living in the East End of London beating a hammer against an anvil in his shop at 30 Hanbury Street. It was next door to where the body of Annie Chapman, Jack the Ripper's second victim, was found. Karayan was not Jack the Ripper, but he claimed to know who it was. "My lips are sealed by fear." That's all he said when questioned. "It's more than my life's worth to reveal the true identity of Jack the Ripper."

Nobody in the Vamp-Art Café doubted him. He was not a vampire prone to ego, exaggeration, or flights of fancy. If he said he knew the identity of Jack the Ripper, then he knew the identity of Jack the Ripper. "All I'll say is this, Jack the Ripper was not a vampire. However, she was of royal blood. A carrier of hemophilia. Look to the daughters in the palace for Jackie the Ripper. I've already said too much." All hints pointed to Jack the Ripper being Princess Louise, the Duchess of Argyle.

Karayan stepped onto the stage. "This story is called, *I Am the Girl with a Pearl Earring painted by Johannes Vermeer.*"

Karayan recited the story from memory. He had told it many times before.

TWO

I AM THE GIRL WITH THE PEARL EARRING PAINTED BY JOHANNES VERMEER

A Tale Told by Edwin Karayan

At sixteen-years-of-age the life of Lady Sarah Frigginsaw was one of privilege and wealth. Within the strictures of Britain's class system, that was her birthright. Her entitlement. However, Lady Sarah was a disappointment. She didn't fit the role. She was poisonous belladonna growing in the neatly tended herbaceous borders of Britain's minor aristocracy. In short, she was unsuited to be the daughter of Viscount Timothy Frigginsaw and his wife, Viscountess Mary Frigginsaw (Rococo-Coco to her friends and paramours. Why Rococo-Coco? Nobody knew). The problem was that with privilege comes responsibility, and Lady Sarah wanted none of it. She was gypsy-wild with piercing electric-blue eyes and auburn hair dancing down her back like waves on a desert shore. She resembled a woman on the cover of a Penny Dreadful, running along a clifftop fleeing a haunted mansion and a terrible marriage. Behind her, lightning strikes a manor house with an attic inhabited by spider webs, birds' nests, bats, ghosts, and raving lunatics. And yet, everybody loved Lady Sarah: cuckoos tried to lay eggs in her hair; bees wanted to nest in her skull; gray-whiskered suicidal badgers longed to curl up and die in her lap. Lady Sarah was a red-blooded woman, not a blue-blooded ballerina in a glass-domed music box. She did not pirouette wearing a pretty-in-pink tutu accompanied by the tinkling of Tchaikovsky's *Dance of the Sugar Plum Fairy*. No, Lady Sarah Frigginsaw eagerly awaited the storm she knew was headed her way.

Although uttered only in whispers, Lady Sarah's parentage was the subject of feverish gossip and speculation. She was undoubtedly the daughter of Viscountess Frigginsaw. The whole county heard the screams the night Lady Sarah was born. The windows of Frigginsaw House were open, and Rococo-Coco's curses crawled across the fields and copses like mustard gas. "This child is tearing me apart!" … "I am rent in twain!" … "Fuck this bastard child!" No, there was no doubt Lady Sarah fell from Viscountess Mary's womb. It was the identity of her father that was in doubt. It was rumored the Viscount's passions were sated in the Molly houses of London. It was said his "roundmouth" was repeatedly violated by youths who gut cod at Billingsgate Fish Market. It was also known that Rococo-Coco rutted like a whore with all and sundry. Lady Sarah's real father was any of the male staff living in two rows of tied cottages in Winscombe Fields near the stables.

Lady Sarah bore a striking resemblance to Arthur Strubb, the head gardener, or any of his six sons. The child wasn't Arthur's as he was a pious churchgoer, cursing and fornication alien to him. It was more likely one of his sons as Rococo-Coco had mounted them all. Including Grahame Strubb, the youngest, thirteen years of age at the time of Lady Sarah's conception. And he wasn't the youngest to slide his whore-pipe into her crinkum-crankum. Rococo-Coco also drained the tallywags of Edward, the blacksmith's twelve-year-old son. The boy was swimming naked in the river. Rococo-Coco, seeing his pubescent erect member, pushed him onto the grassy bank, mounted him and rode him like a hobbyhorse. The boy thought they were wrestling. She gave him a shiny sixpence for his trouble.

Frigginsaw House was a fifteen-bedroom mansion in 300 acres of grounds, sandwiched between the Thames River and Northbrooke Woods. It was near Piddledick Crumpet, a hamlet of twenty houses, St. Michael's church, and a post office and grocery store run by Agnes Bell, a frosty-faced spinster with a distracting speech impediment. Lady Sarah's favorite childhood memory was of riverbank picnics with Jane Orwin, her nanny. Orwin was only in her thirties at the time but to Lady Sarah she was as old as the lanes and hedgerows, as ancient as dirt and the roots of oak trees. The Lady and her nanny sat cross-legged on a tartan blanket stretched out on the grass with a basket of bread, cheese, barley water, and an apple. It was Orwin who taught Lady Sarah the names of the plants: the yellow gorse, St. John's-wort, penny-wort, gypsy-wort and water mint. Orwin also knew the names of local birds: the nightjar, Dartford warbler, and woodlark. The nightjars appeared at twilight hunting moths, wings V-shaped and clapping, tail feather fanned out, their call a churring sound, not unlike a frog trapped in a box.

"The nightjar suckles milk from the titties of goats." Orwin was famous for her Old Wives' Tales. "Come morning those goat titties are dry. Dry as parchment." Another of Orwin's tales involved hair. If a person's hair is cut with the moon on the wane, it loses its luster. Orwin also read moles and dimples: on the left side of the body – unlucky, on the right – lucky; a mole on the nose – great treachery; on a woman's thigh – unfaithful; a dimple on the chin, the Devil within; and warts – the evilest of all. Lady

Sarah wanted to believe her nanny's tales, but she didn't. She did try, though.

Lady Sarah was kept isolated, sheltered from worldly influences, like Rapunzel imprisoned in an ivy-covered tower, a linnet in a gilded cage, a butterfly pinned to a board. The young aristocrat was home-tutored by Donald Simden, a gangly creature with a body like twisted wire. He wore pince-nez perched on his nose and colorful waistcoats. He cracked his fingers like dead twigs and was a lascivious creature with myriad perversions. Among his odd interests were an obsession with feet, women's silk dress slippers, singing hymns with a bucket on his head, rubbing his testicles against corduroy, and igniting gas from his anus with a lit taper. He taught Lady Sarah rudimentary math, English, history, and geography, enough to engage her, but not enough to think herself equal to men. He often asked Lady Sarah to retrieve books from high shelves in the library in order to look up her skirt. In an unspoken agreement, she sometimes fetched books from the upper shelves *sans* underwear. She stretched to reach Jane Austen's *Pride and Prejudice* while lifting her skirt and parting her legs, revealing a virgin crack, a woman's smile on a pair of mute, quivering, lips. On those days Simden stared admiringly for a while, excused himself, and lessons were over for the day. While he busied himself in the water closet, Lady Sarah escaped down a back staircase. In the garden, she turned into the Avenue of Poplars, jumped a fence, then ran through shady Northbrooke Woods to the boathouse. She was Boudica the Celtic warrior Queen ridding Britain of the Romans, knives spinning on the wheels of her chariot, a Gáe Bulg, a spear of death, gripped in her tiny white hand. Woe betides any foolish soul who came within reach. She would cut them down without thinking twice about it.

At the boathouse, Lady Sarah untied a small craft and rowed to the midstream of the Thames river. Tugging her hat down over her face she peered under the brim at moorhens, coots, and great crested grebes bobbing on the water. A heron guarded her eggs on the far bank and a water vole dug a nest in a bed of reeds. The boat drifted. Lady Sarah imagined herself nomadic, a gypsy traveling English country lanes in a vardo, a Bedouin tribeswoman wrapped in rugs and incense on bitter cold Sahara nights in a tent. Lady Sarah had no faith in Bibles or the morals and meanderings of men, only the pagan power of the tides and the wind. Instinctively Wiccan, she was closer to nature – drizzling rain, damp soil, and wet grass – than the pomp and prejudice of the Church of England. On those balmy summer days afloat on the river, Lady Sarah transformed herself into an electric-blue dragonfly, glittering in the sunlight, hovering over the water, pretty and unpredictable in equal measure.

On this particular day Lady Sarah satisfied Simden's lecherous gaze, bolted down the back stairs, through the garden, across open fields until she reached a country lane. There, she sat on a dry-stone wall and opened Emily Bronte's *Wuthering Heights*. She read the first line out loud. "1801. - I have just returned from a visit to my landlord - the solitary neighbour that I shall be troubled with. This is certainly a beautiful country!"

The wall marked the boundary of the Frigginsaw estate. It was originally built by Roman conquerors in the reign of Emperor Septimus Severus. As Sarah absorbed the passionate love throes of Cathy and Heathcliff, she broke off to bid "good morning" to laborers heading for the fields and barns. Some old, wizened, their faces carved from granite, others younger, virile, their muscular arms like hams. Some she recognized, others not. A rickety cart pulled up alongside her. It was piled high with potatoes and pulled by a mixed-blood cob, coat as black as jet, nostrils flaring, hooves pawing at the ground. Driving the cart, a boy of fifteen or so wore threadbare clothes and boots. The sole of his right boot was tied on with rope. His blond fringe fell into his eyes and he lifted his battered cap and swept back his hair using his fingers as a comb. "Do you need a lift? I'm heading for Upton Inglesbatch."

"Yes, thank you." Lady Sarah climbed into the seat alongside him. She left her copy of *Wuthering Heights* on the dry-stone wall. Perhaps a stranger needed to read it more than she did.

"My name is Robert, Robert Glumm." The youth grinned. Birds sang. Baby rabbits hopped for joy. Petals unfolded on roses. The whole world lit up.

"I'm Sarah."

A little up the lane, the cart passed a pair of tall, wrought-iron gates, that opened onto the driveway to Frigginsaw House.

"Who lives in that house?" Robert pointed to Lady Sarah's home on the hill.

"I don't know." Lady Sarah shrugged her shoulders and stared straight ahead. "Nobody I know."

Lady Sarah resisted the urge to glance back at Frigginsaw House with its fountains, topiary, and tall brick chimney stacks. She feared turning into a pillar of salt like Lot's wife looking back at Sodom. Instinctively, Lady Sarah knew she would never see Frigginsaw House again – a gut feeling. A thrill and a chill shot through her thin frame as the cart entered the dark and dense Northbrooke Woods. Here lived foxes, badgers, and pine martens, among the wood anemones, blackberry brambles, and wild garlic. In a shady tunnel of hazelnut trees, Lady Sarah laughed as Robert sang a popular Music Hall song:

> *Hello! Hello! Who's your lady friend?*
> *Who's the little girlie by your side?*
> *I've seen you with a girl or two.*

Oh! Oh! Oh! I am, surprised at you;
Hello! Hello! Stop your little games.
Don't you think your ways
You ought to mend?
It isn't the girl I saw you with at Uvongo
Who? Who? Who's your lady friend?

It wasn't long before Lady Sarah learned the words. They sang the song together over and over again as the cart snaked through fields of bluebells, over stone humpback bridges, and along picturesque English country lanes. In Upton Inglesbatch, Lady Sarah thanked and bid farewell to Robert. She stepped down from the cart onto the dusty cobbled high street on a hill lined with shops on either side. On one side, a butcher, milliner, teashop, ladies' dress shop, and sweet shop with jars of bull's eyes, pear drops, humbugs, and licorice sticks. On the other, a grocer, post office, fishmonger, tobacconist, and blacksmith. As Robert's cart pulled away, a raven's feather floated on the breeze. Lady Sarah tried to catch it, but it wafted over a hedge. Ra, the orange spong, shone in the sky like an orange, waiting to be peeled and eaten later by the fangs of twilight. The sharp, irritating chatter of children filled the air. Lunch break over, a class of students filed into a one-room schoolhouse called Inglesbatch Infants School. The teacher, a Mrs. Edna Marchmilitant, stood at the door calling names and checking them off a list … Cynthia Squadrill … John Higginbottom … Emily Cordwangler … Simon Thorn. The children, each with a leather satchel slung over their shoulder, carried chalk and slates on which to write.

This was Lady Sarah's second visit to Upton Inglesbatch. She came once before with Jane Orwin, her beloved nanny. The church, St. Swithin's, is where her grandparents, Viscount David Frigginsaw and Viscountess Alexandra Frigginsaw, lay interned in a mausoleum. The gothic marble box with sinister, grinning, gargoyle guttering stood next to a yew tree with spiky needles and poisonous red berries, in a secluded area of the churchyard. Why were Lady Sarah's grandparents buried in Upton Inglesbatch when generations of Frigginsaws rested at St. Michael's in Piddledick Crumpet? It was due to a feud between the Frigginsaw family and the late Rev. George Lashwood, former vicar at St. Michael's. Details were vague, but there was a scandal with the vicar, involving a bottle of wine, two choirboys, a scented candle from the Chapel of St. Dorothy, and deep gashes in the walls of the rectory. Whatever the indiscretion, it was so bad the Frigginsaws couldn't find it within themselves to forgive it. When Lady Sarah's grandparents passed away, soon afterwards they were buried in Upton Inglesbatch as a protest. Two years after the incident, Rev. Lashwood died in a freak gardening accident – he was singing *All Things Bright and Beautiful* when he stepped on a rake. It struck him in the forehead, and he tumbled headfirst into a freshly dug grave. Three days later, at the funeral of Marcia Steppenthorpe – midwife in the parish – Rev. Lashwood was found stiff as a board, dead from hypothermia.

On her first visit to Upton Inglesbatch, Lady Sarah and her nanny didn't enter the mausoleum. It was dark, dank, and creepy. On that bleak chilly autumn afternoon, they stood outside of it as crisp dead leaves fell from the trees like confetti at a zombie wedding. The leaves formed a damp brown, green, and red carpet at their feet. That was over two years ago. Soon after that visit to Upton Inglesbatch, nanny married a carpenter and moved to the south coast. Now Lady Sarah was back in this village-on-a-hill. This time, she was alone. This time, she had no reason to be there. This time, she was a wandering gypsy girl, a dragonfly, a raven's feather on the breeze.

Lady Sarah climbed the hill to St. Swithin's, not to visit her family tomb or seek succor from God, but to savor a moment of solitude in the church. She pushed open the creaking gate and walked up the path to the heavy oak door with its iron hinges and handle. Inside, Lady Sarah slid into a pew. Above the altar a stained-glass window depicted a suffering Christ on the cross. The rays from Ra, the orange spong, penetrated the translucent glass, dancing on the Lord's lips, quivering, flickering, and shimmering. Christ was speaking; and Lady Sarah listened. His voice was high-pitched and reminded her of a puppet. She recalled the time her father hired Teatro de Marionetas to entertain at her tenth birthday party. In the play, a donkey puppet ate a carrot. Christ sounded like that donkey. Christ was braying, "Buy cheese for Mary Magdalene. Buy cheese for Mary Magdalene." The Son of God repeated it over and over again, "Buy cheese for Mary Magdalene" … that's what it sounded like, anyway. It made no sense.

Lady Sarah fled the church to escape Christ's mantra … "Buy cheese for Mary Magdalene." It jarred her nerves. She skillfully navigated the rows of graves, skipped down the gravel path and out through the lychgate. She leaned against a mossy wall to collect her thoughts. As a flock of honking geese flew over the rooftops of a nearby row of thatched cottages, a calèche pulled up alongside her. A man wearing a black coat, top hat, and a rakish mustache introduced himself. "I am Chez Tortoni painted by Édouard Manet. Are you Lady Sarah Frigginsaw? Of course you are! Who else would you be? Climb inside."

"Is that your real name? Chez Tortoni painted by Édouard Manet doesn't sound like a name. Not a sensible name, anyway."

The driver of the calèche ignored the question and stared straight ahead. There was an awkward silence. Somewhere in the distance a sparrow died mid-flight, floating to the floor with a dull thud. A thud heard only by other sparrows and felt by earthworms – earthworms feel everything. Lady Sarah hesitated, then shrugged and climbed into the cab. She was not afraid. Fear is an indulgence, a trap. Fear is a luxury the inquisitive can't afford.

With the leather springs of the calèche squeaking, Chez Tortoni painted by Édouard Manet drove Lady Sarah through a beech wood, cornfields, and meadows of wild primroses, cowslips, and moon daisies. Three miles up the road they turned into a driveway, past a hand-painted wooden sign reading Manticore House. It hung crooked, dangling on two rusting chains. They continued along an avenue of majestic rhododendron bushes – clusters of pink, red, white, and yellow blooms. Eventually the calèche pulled up at the door of a crumbling 16th century Tudor mansion with pitched gable roofs, elaborate chimneys, half-timbering, and an exposed wood frame. A woman wearing a mobcap with a blue ribbon around it waited like a statue. Her skin was bleached white. It was twilight now, Ra, the orange spong, a soft warm glow on the horizon. A sedge warbler sang in the distance. Swarms of gnats rolled over the fields toward Longstocking Woods, where the rumored ghost of a highwayman rode at midnight.

The bleached-white woman opened the calèche door and smiled. "Ah! There you are, Lady Sarah Frigginsaw. Come in, I'll show you to your room. We've been expecting you." The woman smiled and wiped her hands on her apron. "Be careful as you enter the house, it's being eaten away by neglect. Neglect is the hungriest of creatures, don't you think?"

Lady Sarah remained silent – she had no answer to the question. She followed the woman to the door of Manticore House, rotting on its hinges, a victim of years of inclement weather, rust and woodworm. It was jammed open. Lady Sarah squeezed through the gap into the large hallway.

Somewhere in its past, Manticore House opened itself up to the elements. The outside was invited in, and it accepted the offer with great enthusiasm – the hallway was strewn with leaves, branches and pinecones. A tree grew through the quarry-tiled floor, its roots visible, its branches shattering windows up in the stairwell. Above her head, Lady Sarah heard the grunting, squeaking, and chattering of monkeys. Bats hung from the bannisters. A miniature pot-bellied pig scurried across the floor. And, in the distance, an elephant trumpeted.

"Don't be alarmed, Lady Sarah. Manticore House has long been a zoo without cages. The animals run free here. 'The Master' wants it this way."

"Who's 'The Master?'"

The question hung suspended in the air unanswered. At Manticore House unanswered questions dangle like icicles from parapets, 'til they become too heavy, snap off, fall, and shatter into a thousand pieces on the ground below. Unanswered questions cling tightly to walls like barnacles on the wooden hull of a pirate ship. In this Tudor mansion you will find unanswered questions stuffed into bureau drawers, knotted up with balls of string and bunches of keys to forgotten doors. In the bedrooms, unanswered questions hang neatly on coat hangers in closets or lay wadded up on filthy floors with only discarded clothes for company. Sometimes unanswered questions curl up immediately after leaving someone's lips, wither and die, unheard.

The strange woman with a blue ribbon attached to her mobcap climbed the grand staircase, her skirt hitched up with one hand, a kerosene carriage lamp dangling from the other. Lady Sarah followed along behind, kicking aside twigs, brambles and bracken strewn across the stairs like booby traps. Up in the stairwell she saw silhouettes of monkeys swinging in and out of broken windows. An owl swooped and flew past her head with a struggling mouse in its talons. A badger eyed her suspiciously from behind a suit of armor.

"My name is Woman Knitting painted by Francoise Duparc." After two flights of stairs the bleached woman stopped to catch her breath. "Your room is in here. If you need anything, please ring the bell. Dinner will be in one hour. You'll hear the gong. The dining room is downstairs."

Woman Knitting painted by Francoise Duparc motioned Lady Sarah into a large bedroom, then turned, descended the stairs, and was gone like a will-o'-the-wisp. A kookaburra's laugh cut the air like a scimitar. A single candle flame flickered on a nightstand. Shadows danced on the walls, frenetic and hyper like children lost in the woods trying to find their way home. Lady Sarah pulled back the drapes and peered out the window. It was dark, but she detected the silhouettes of giraffes striding across the untended grounds. A lion roared. A pigeon landed on the window ledge. Exhausted, Lady Sarah stretched out on the bed and slept. Her light snores fascinated a bush baby sitting on the mantelpiece over the fireplace. He jumped onto the bed and tried to feed Lady Sarah a grape. He pushed the grape into her mouth, but she spat it out and sleepily brushed him aside. Sometime later, she woke to the sound of a distant gong. Wiping sleep from her eyes, she struggled down the staircase in almost total darkness, one careful step at a time. As she did so, she closed her eyes tightly, preferring blackness to the eerie shadows of wild things lurking in the half-light. As she stepped onto the floor at the bottom of the stairs, she opened her eyes. Woman Knitting painted by Francoise Duparc stood in the shadows nearby. Lady Sarah found the woman's presence strangely comforting. She sensed a kindred spirit, a camaraderie, not friendship exactly, but a kinship born of a shared history – both were victims of circumstances beyond their control.

"Lady Sarah, please come this way."

In the dining room, Lady Sarah sat in a Queen Anne dining chair at a long mahogany table set for thirteen guests. The room was lit by dozens of candles standing on every available flat surface. Yet, still it was dark.

"Am I to dine alone?" Lady Sarah pushed back her hair.

"No, the other guests will be here soon."

Woman Knitting painted by Francoise Duparc left the room. Lady Sarah sat alone with the flickering candlelight dancing tangoes of filigree and shadow across her delicate face. Her thoughts turned to her parents. Her memory of them was fading. Her mother's face was a blur, her father's clearer, though his nose and mouth had gone. For Lady Sarah the past was vanishing, a rambunctious voice withering to a whisper. Her reverie was interrupted by a scratching sound. It was a squirrel on the back of an armchair chewing a peanut. His tail twitched as they locked eyes. Something primeval passed between them. Raw. Animal. Also, a fox hid under a sideboard, trembling, whiskers twitching, eyes nervously scanning the room for danger and an escape route. An open fire crackled in the hearth – logs glowing, sparks flying. On the walls hung heavy tapestries depicting long-gone medieval battles fought over greed and papal supremacy. Bodies, pierced by arrows and spears, lay strewn before castle walls, on the high battlements, and on blood-soaked battlefields. A bishop, his cassock dripping with blood, held up a tall cross, triumphantly, even though an arrow pierced his eye and another his heart.

In spite of the unfamiliar and strange surroundings, Lady Sarah felt relaxed, drugged almost, a somnambulist stumbling through a dreamscape. A woman drifted into the dining room. Lady Sarah recognized her, though she couldn't say from where. It was on the tip of her tongue. The woman had long dark hair, a strange smile, eyebrows and eyelashes plucked. She wore a green velvet dress and a veil draped across her head. The woman wiped a strand of hair from her face, a bisque porcelain doll's face. Then she placed her large hands on the table, fingers folded like knotted tree roots.

"My name is Sarah. I'm very pleased to meet you." Lady Sarah stood up and held out her hand. It was ignored.

A full minute passed before the woman spoke. "My name is Mona Lisa painted by Leonardo da Vinci." The woman sputtered out the words as if they tasted of bitter almonds. Her fingers fluttered on the dining table as if tickling piano keys. Her nose lifted up into the air. "I don't know who you are, but I feel I must make this perfectly clear from the beginning. I hated being painted. My husband wanted it. He wanted my image to live forever. Nothing lives forever, only vampires and dangerous paths through dark fairy tale forests. Now I am both of those things."

Lady Sarah now recognized her. She once saw the Mona Lisa painting in a book. A raven landed on the shoulder of Mona Lisa painted by Leonardo da Vinci. "Ah, Mr. Raven, how is your wing? I hope that it's mended." Then turning to Sarah, she explained. "Mr. Raven flew into one of the chimneys here. Crashed into it. He was thinking about something else and wasn't looking where he was going. Silly bird. I found him lying in the garden with a damaged wing. I sang to him and nursed him back to health. Now he will live for all eternity."

"What song did you sing?" Lady Sarah was curious and determined to open a conversation.

"*Osculetur me* by Giovanni Pierluigi da Palestrina." Mona Lisa painted by Leonardo da Vinci began to sing. "*Oh se mi baciasse con i baci della sua bocca! Davvero i tuoi seni sono migliori del vino, profumati di ottimi unguenti. Essenza che si espande è il tuo nome: per questo le giovinette sono innamorate di te. Attirami a te! Correremo all'odore dei tuoi profumi. Il re mi ha introdotto nelle sue stanze. Gioiremo e godremo di te, avidi dei tuoi seni più che del vino. I giusti ti vogliono bene.*"

"Can you sing it in English?" Enchanted by the melody, Lady Sarah longed to hear the words in a language she understood.

"Yes, I can. *Let him kiss me with the kiss of his mouth: for thy breasts are better than wine, smelling sweet of the best ointments. Thy name is as oil poured out: therefore young maidens have loved thee.*"

"How is Mr. Raven?" A blue-skinned, sleepy-eyed woman, with an avalanche of lopsided hair, and pouting lips, interrupted. "He seems better. His wing looks healed." She didn't wait or an answer. "I see we have a guest."

"My name is Sarah."

"I am very pleased to meet you, Sarah. I am Woman with Her Hair in a Small Bun painted by Pablo Picasso."

They shook hands briefly, but Lady Sarah quickly pulled away. There was a slight electric shock. "Oh, my goodness! What was that? Are you electric?"

"Oh, I'm sorry, I do apologize. I shouldn't have shaken your hand. You may or may not know this but the inhabitants of Manticore House are pure energy. We are nothing more than sparks. No, I apologize for shaking your hand. Old habits die hard." Woman with Her Hair in a Small Bun painted by Pablo Picasso smiled and bowed her head slightly.

Lady Sarah experienced a moment of realization, satori, a sudden awareness – a lightbulb went on. She was unfamiliar with Pablo Picasso but surmised he was an artist and Woman with Her Hair in a Small Bun painted by Pablo Picasso modeled for one of his paintings. Something of the *modus operandi* at Manticore House was revealed – the inhabitants of this dilapidated Tudor mansion all posed for portraits in paintings. It was all very odd. Lady Sarah was intrigued.

"Where is everyone?" Woman with Her Hair in a Small Bun painted by Pablo Picasso sat opposite Lady Sarah. "Would you mind if I sat here, I want to look at your hair? It reminds me of dark velvet curtains in a Parisian funeral parlor, shielding a corpse, a cadaver soon to take up residence at Cimetière du Père Lachaise. Your hair makes me think of *Thérèse Raquin*, the novel by Émile Zola, but I don't know why. Perhaps it's because I can see you naked on a mortuary slab."

Lady Sarah remained silent. She briefly felt that she was drowning.

"I'm sure the others will be here soon." Mona Lisa painted by Leonardo da Vinci kissed the raven's beak. The bird coughed-up a volley of gurgling croaks then flew into the hallway and perched on a grandfather clock. "Look, the raven wants to know what time it is."

"That clock doesn't work." Woman with Her Hair in a Small Bun painted by Pablo Picasso laughed and called out to the raven, "It doesn't work. The monkeys tore off the hands and pendulum months ago. Time stopped."

"Time hasn't stopped, it lies in the gutter bleeding." A new guest joined them at the table. This woman wore a kimono, carried a fan, and introduced herself as Lady with Fan painted by Gustav Klimt. "So, who are you?"

Lady Sarah extended her hand, then remembering the electric shock she received earlier, pulled it back quickly. "My name is Sarah."

"Ah, yes, I vaguely remember now. I was told you were coming. Do you think my cheeks are too red? Be honest with me. Do I look like a Geisha? What do you think, tell me what you think? I have to know what people think."

"I think you're beautiful, hair as black as it should be, cheeks and lips as red as they need to be. No more, no less. You were painted perfectly." Lady Sarah leaned back in her chair and folded her arms across her chest.

"Mr. Klimt thought I was Japanese. I'm not. That's the problem with Austrian symbolists, they think everyone is Japanese."

"Oh, that's just not true." Mona Lisa painted by Leonardo da Vinci brushed the idea aside. "It's nonsense. Not all Austrian symbolists think everyone is Japanese, just Gustav Klimt."

Lady Sarah relaxed with her new friends. Lady with Fan painted by Gustav Klimt was the most beautiful woman she had ever seen. The Mona Lisa painted by Leonardo da Vinci, the most peculiar, and Woman with Her Hair in a Small Bun painted by Pablo Picasso, the most amusing. For a moment, Lady Sarah tried again to remember her parents' faces, but now they were hidden under death shrouds with veils. Which of these veils hid her mother's face, which her father's? Lady Sarah's thoughts were shattered by a 1,500 lbs. Sumatran rhinoceros stampeding through the hallway, toppling a hall stand and causing other animals to run for cover. Chimpanzees seized upon the hats, coats, and umbrellas on the hallstand and dragged them away.

"Well who needs umbrellas?" Woman with Her Hair in a Small Bun painted by Pablo Picasso shrugged and laughed. "Umbrellas are for cowards, people frightened of rain. Who are these people who fear wet feet and the patter of raindrops?"

"Umbrellas should only be used by people attending funerals." A woman in a black mourning dress, carrying a nosegay of violets, joined the others at the table. She introduced herself as Berthe Moriot with a Bouquet of Violets painted by Édouard Manet. "And they should always be black umbrellas. Not blue or pink but black. I've said it before and I'll say it again, colored umbrellas are an abomination, the work of Satan. I have very definite opinions on the subject of umbrellas, and I will not be swayed from those opinions."

Other guests entered the dining room like treacle trickling from a spoon: Woman with Red Hair painted by Amedeo Modigliani; Portrait of the Empress Eugenie painted by Franz Xavier Winterhalter; Beata Beatrix painted by Dante Gabriel Rossetti; Portrait of Doctor Félix Rey painted by Vincent Van Gogh; Orphan Girl at the Cemetery painted by Eugene Dalacroix; Duke of Buccleuch With His Dog painted by Thomas Gainsborough; and Damenporträt painted by Emil von Gerliczy.

One seat at the head of the table remained empty. Beata Beatrix painted by Dante Gabriel Rossetti peered down at the bird sitting in her lap. "Where is 'The Master' tonight?"

"He will be joining us later in the gallery." Damenporträt painted by Emil von Gerliczy removed her hatpins and placed her large pink plumed hat on the sideboard. "He said he is busy."

"Well I am hungry." Orphan Girl at the Cemetery painted by Eugene Delacroix, a thin waiflike creature in a peasant blouse with uneven stitching, placed her hands on her hips. "I could eat a horse."

The room fell silent and a black cloud descended. After a few seconds, Damenporträt painted by Emil von Gerliczy broke the silence. "When you say you could eat a horse, you mean a mortal horse. Not a vampire horse. Not a horse that we have granted everlasting life."

"Of course not. We only eat that which fears death. Those creatures who are finite. Those who expect their life to end." Orphan Girl at the Cemetery painted by Eugene Delacroix blushed.

"You're always hungry. You've got hollow legs." Damenporträt painted by Emil von Gerliczy laughed. "You're a baby bird in a nest, beak open … beep … beep … beep. Feed me, mother, feed me."

The dinner party was interrupted by a loud crash. Shards of broken glass spit through the air, some landing on the dining table, others skidded across the floor. A giraffe's head pushed through the freshly-broken window. The animal was drooling, a foot-long string of spittle dribbled from his lips. "Ah my friend is coming to visit me." Damenporträt painted by Emil von Gerliczy ran to the window and petted the giraffe's head. "Lady Sarah, meet my friend. It's no secret that I have an affinity with giraffes. I'm sorry, Mr. Giraffe, I don't have a carrot to give you today."

"Give him one of your shoes. Giraffe's just adore shoes." Portrait of the Empress Eugenie painted by Franz Xavier Winterhalter was clinically insane, completely mad, barmy but harmless. If she hadn't been a vampire steam robot, she'd be wearing a straitjacket in a lunatic asylum, babbling about poltergeists, lemongrass, and pots of honey. Pulling her wrap around her shoulders, the Empress shivered in this cavernous dining hall. "I'm sorry, you must excuse my outburst. I have recently discovered rabbits living in my undergarments."

Lady Sarah raised her eyebrows. "That must have been extremely uncomfortable for you. How many rabbits did you have there?"

"Dozens."

"How tedious." Lady Sarah smiled. "I would find rabbits in my undergarments to be very annoying."

Woman Knitting painted by Francoise Duparc returned from the kitchen carrying a silver tureen. She placed the dish on the sideboard next to a splattering of raven poop. Portrait of Félix Rey painted by Vincent Van Gogh unfolded his napkin, then laid it on his lap. "And what is the soup tonight? I hope it's not mock turtle. I hate mock turtle soup."

Woman Knitting painted by Francoise Duparc ladled soup into bowls. "Tonight, we have cream of broccoli soup, followed by braised pheasant with cider and apples and peach galette for dessert."

"Ah, a feast!" Portrait of Doctor Félix Rey painted by Vincent Van Gogh raised his eyes to the ceiling. "Praise God!"

"I thought you were a non-believer." Beata Beatrix painted by Dante Gabriel Rossetti challenged him. "I've heard you say so on many occasions. I have even heard you curse God's name."

"So have I." Damenporträt painted by Emil von Gerliczy adjusted her earrings. "I've heard you say, 'to hell with God.'"

"Yes, I may have said that. But now, presented with such a feast, I praise God for this wondrous bounty. Or I would praise him if he existed, which, of course, he doesn't." Portrait of Doctor Félix Rey painted by Vincent Van Gogh laughed loudly, his eyes twinkling, two black pearls on an olive-colored plate. "I am, of course, talking about the Judeo-Christian God, not Ra, the orange spong, who most certainly does exist and is our creator. Though I doubt that Ra would consider himself to be a god."

"All this talk of Gods existing or not existing, have we forgotten why we are here tonight?" Woman with Red Hair painted by Amedeo Modigliani slammed her fist on the table. "The date is April 31st, and this is the feast before Valpurgijos naktis – a time when witches and sorcerers meet. Also vampires."

"Yes, you are correct. We must not forget why we are here. We are here to drain away the fear of death. We are here to create an immortal." The Duke of Buccleuch With His Dog painted by Thomas Gainsborough tucked his napkin into his stiff collar. He petted his drooling mutt, sitting loyally at his feet. "It seems strange that 'The Master' is not here, on such an auspicious night."

The portraits fell silent during the soup course, conversation picking up with the braised pheasant. "I knew this pheasant. I knew this pheasant well." Berthe Morisot with a Bouquet of Violets painted by Édouard Manet laughed. "I often saw this pheasant strutting in the grounds."

"Did the pheasant have a name?" Damenporträt painted by Emil von Gerliczy pushed a slice of meat to the side of her plate.

"No, it didn't."

"It's too late to give it a name now." Damenporträt painted by Emil von Gerliczy pushed the plate away. "I don't think I can eat this."

"It's never too late to name a pheasant." Orphan Girl at the Cemetery painted by Eugene Delacroix interrupted. She rarely spoke but she was passionate about naming things. She owned a teapot called Peter the Great of Russia and a chamber pot called Pope Sergius III. "Everything should be named, because even mortal pheasants deserve a name. I'm going to name this pheasant Squirmwood."

"Well I have to say that Squirmwood is quite delicious." Portrait of Doctor Félix Rey painted by Vincent Van Gogh laughed. He waved a slice of pheasant on his fork. "It looks like a Squirmwood. It looks squirmy and wooden."

Damenporträt painted by Emil von Gerliczy placed her plate on the floor. The fox under the sideboard ran to it and gobbled up the pheasant. "Now it's got a name, I can't eat it. I'm going vegetarian."

"I'll eat the pheasant. It doesn't bother me at all. The pheasant knew that it was mortal, that it would die." Portrait of the Empress Eugenie painted by Franz Xavier Winterhalter sliced the meat on her plate. "We all have to eat. That's the way of things for us now. We are no longer living in paradise with Ra, the orange spong. We now live among the mortals."

Lady Sarah was transfixed. All this talk of Ra, orange spongs, mortals and immortals, confused her. Nothing made any sense. While the portraits ate dinner, several bottles of Recas Castle Cabernet Sauvignon, a Transylvanian wine, were sipped and commented on. Then after dessert, coffee, and topics of conversation ranging from bees, jugglers, the sex life of antelopes, to Vikings and cuckoo clocks, the guests folded their napkins, tossed them onto the table and filed out of the dining room. In pairs and trios, they promenaded down a corridor, past squawking parrots, strutting peacocks and a sounder of warthogs. Leading the procession, Mona Lisa painted by Leonardo da Vinci carried a lantern and hummed a sad Russian folk song softly under her breath.

"I thought the peach galette was excellent." Woman with Her Hair in a Small Bun painted by Pablo Picasso confided in Portrait of Doctor Félix Rey painted by Vincent Van Gogh. "However, the cream of broccoli soup lacked a certain something, but I don't know what."

"It needed celery."

"Yes, celery would have improved it greatly."

As the procession continued down the corridor, staff members at Manticore House joined the end of the line. First Woman Knitting painted by Francoise Duparc, then calèche driver Chez Tortoni painted by Édouard Manet. The portraits entered a library, then filed out through another door and down another corridor. Portrait of Doctor Félix Rey painted by Vincent Van Gogh stopped to tie his shoelace. "I hate shoelaces almost as much as I hate sailors."

"Sailors? What's wrong with sailors?" Woman with Red Hair painted by Amedeo Modigliani brushed cobwebs from her clothes.

"What's wrong with sailors? Don't get me started on that subject. I won't be able to stop." Portrait of Doctor Félix Rey painted by Vincent Van Gogh finished tying his shoelace, then rejoined the procession.

At the bottom of a staircase leading up into the servants' bedrooms, more staff joined the parade. They introduced themselves to Lady Sarah as Boy with a Basket of Fruit painted by Michelangelo Merisi da Caravaggio; Penitent Mary Magdalene painted by Tiziano Vecellio; Boreas painted by John William Waterhouse; Portrait of Moise Kisling painted by Amedeo Modigliani; Portrait of Eleonora Gonzaga della Rovere painted by Tiziano Vecellio; Portrait of a Young Woman painted by Sandro Botticelli; and Portrait of a Young Venetian Woman painted by Albrecht Durer.

When Battle of Balaclava Drummer Boy painted by Richard Buckner joined the procession, it became a military march. Rat-a-tat-tat. Rat-a-tat-tat. Rat-a-tat-tat. Rat-a-tat-tat. Rat-a-tat-tat. Rat-a-tat-tat. The portraits fell into lockstep, marching up staircases, along hallways, past zebras in corridors, flamingos on landings and owls nesting in attics. Eventually the troops filed into a cavernous baronial hall with a wood fire burning at one end. A row of empty picture frames lined the walls. Each bore a plaque with the title of a painting and the name of the artist. The portraits tore off their faces, hung them on hooks, and stepped into their respective frames. Where their faces had been, was now a tangled mass of tubes, cogs, and wheels. These mechanisms released short bursts of steam, gears turned and chugged, and a hammer attached to a wheel ticked like a clock. In the distance an engine hummed. The robot portraits recharged their distribulating fobulosity 4-8 Sound Bowl Cumwiggles and Fattress. They were exhausted, out of steam.

Lady Sarah stood alone. She examined each painting in turn. First, the death mask of Berthe Morisot with a Bouquet of Violets painted by Édouard Manet. Cheeks like sunken graves, eyes brimming with more grief than one person can bear. Morisot, painted at her father's funeral, clutched a barely visible posy of violets in her tiny hands. In the painting, her face-mechanism was a mass of pinions, straps, chains, and clamps. Lady Sarah was mesmerized, but finding herself staring into a clockwork abyss, she snapped out of her reverie and stiffened. Next Lady Sarah studied the limp and expressionless death mask of Damenporträt painted by Emil von Gerliczy. In the painting the woman shivered with the cold, fur coat wrapped around her, hands cozy in a muff. Her face-mechanism blew out a jet of steam every ten seconds. Lady Sarah moved from painting to painting. Next, she studied Portrait of Eleonora Gonzaga della Rovere painted by Tiziano Vecellio. In the painting, Gonzaga, the Duchess of Urbino, grande dame of high culture and the arts, is weighed down with heavy jewelry. Behind her a spaniel eyes the artist coquettishly.

The last picture frame was empty. The plaque read, "Girl with a Pearl Earring painted by Johannes Vermeer." It didn't take a soothsayer to predict what happened next. However, Lady Sarah was still caught by surprise. In all the pageantry of recent events at Manticore House, "The Master" slipped her mind. He was mentioned once or twice at the dinner table, after which he was never spoken of again. Yet now, Lady Sarah sensed him standing behind her. She felt his presence, his hot breath on her neck. She became intoxicated, weak, not drunk, but woozy. "I know you're there." Lady Sarah heard a rustling sound. The walls shook violently. Flocks of birds escaped through broken windows, large mammals stampeded down corridors, moths swarmed around the chandelier with its flickering candles that cast shadows of prancing horses onto the walls.

Lady Sarah turned, to be confronted by a giant romaine lettuce with fangs bared, its leaves flapping like sheets on a washing line in a gusty wind. She stepped backwards, tripped over a tree branch and landed on a bed of rotting leaves, pinecones and acorns. She lay motionless, eyes wide open. The giant romaine lettuce circled her twice, then gently tore at her clothes with its leaves, stem, and fangs.

Her fear subsiding, Lady Sarah succumbed to the lettuce's seduction. She relaxed as waves of yearning washed over her and she tumbled into a dark passion more suited to a dungeon than a feather bed. The lettuce's leaves gently caressed Lady Sarah's skin. They felt like wet feathers. Now naked, Lady Sarah whimpered, opened her legs and held out her arms to the lettuce. "The Master" lay on top of her, nuzzled her ear and kissed her mouth. Moments later, Lady Sarah stiffened as the lettuce pushed a leaf between her legs and into her, then two leaves, then three. Inside, she felt a gushing waterfall. Her mind was locked in a wooden barrel plummeting over Niagara Falls. As "The Master" fucked Lady Sarah, she tore at him with her nails until lettuce juice ran down her hands, then down her arms. This was not a woman and a vegetable making love but two wild beings clawing, dragging each other out of a cesspool of loneliness. That's all sex is, two or more entities hungrily escaping solitude for a few brief moments. "The Master" sank his fangs into Lady Sarah's neck, as waves of orgasms washed over her young body. Slowly, her mortal life faded away and eternal life as a vampire steam robot began. The more the lettuce pumped her with steam, the more she crackled with sparks of pure energy. When the transition was complete, the two lay together, exhausted, gasping for air, both empty and full at the same time. After a minute or so, Lady Sarah stood up, tore off her face, hung it on a hook, and stepped into the painting. She was no longer Lady Sarah Frigginsaw, daughter of Viscount and Viscountess Frigginsaw, but Girl with a Pearl Earring painted by Johannes Vermeer.

She was now immortal. A vampire. From her death mask, Girl with a Pearl Earring painted by Johannes Vermeer examined herself in the painting: the headscarf, the pearl earring, and the face-mechanism of metal rods, screws and pipes carrying steam. Inside of herself, she gurgled and bubbled, filled to the brim with a potent mixture of lightning, rocket-fuel, and the ramblings of mad scientists. She stared out into "The Master's" art gallery, at the monkeys swinging from the drapes, a porcupine skidding across the floor. "The Master" sat up and stared lovingly at Girl with a Pearl Earring painted by Johannes Vermeer. Beads of water flowed from the lettuce, down his leaves and stem, and onto the forest floor, in this, the strangest of art galleries. These were vegetable tears of happiness.

Girl with a Pearl Earring painted by Johannes Vermeer stood in the painting until she was fully charged. When she stepped out again, it was not into Manticore House, but into Johannes Vermeer's messy studio in 17th century Holland.

"Stay still!" Vermeer lost his patience with the servant girl. "I can't paint you if you keep moving."

"I'm doing my best, let me rest awhile." Girl with a Pearl Earring painted by Johannes Vermeer climbed down from the dais and peered out the window into the bustling streets of Delft. From this garret she saw the prickly city of spires, the two most prominent churches, Oude and the Nieuwe, the fortified walls, massive gates, bastions, and watchtowers protecting the city from invasion. Also, she saw the Old Delft River and narrow streets. They were crowded with workers filing into the Delft blue china factories, where they exported crockery to Brabant, Flanders, France, Spain, England and the East Indies.

"What do you see from the window?" Vermeer put down his paintbrush.

"I'm looking at my new world. Did you know that your painting is a portal to another world? A world where I was someone else, Lady Sarah Frigginsaw?"

"Yes, I knew that. That's what artists do, paint portals into other worlds. You look into a painting and it transports you. That's what it's supposed to do. But you didn't belong in that other world. You belong here in Delft, in Holland, in 1665."

"But why?"

Vermeer stabbed the canvas with his paintbrush. "There, now it's finished. You are finished."

"But why?" Girl with a Pearl Earring painted by Johannes Vermeer persisted. "If I belong here, as you say, then why was I in that other world?"

"Because not everyone is born into the right painting. You were born mortal, now you are immortal. You once feared death, now you no longer fear it." Vermeer put down his paintbrush and stepped back to admire his work. "Don't worry, I know you have many questions, all will be revealed to you."

"But when?" Lady Sarah insisted.

Vermeer smiled. "As soon as the paint dries."

THREE

BACK AT THE VAMP-ART CAFÉ

Edwin Karayan finished his story to tremendous applause from the vampires seated in the Vamp-Art Café. Every one of them bared their fangs and wailed like Clíodhna, Irish Fairy Queen of the Banshees. Viorica Negrescu pushed her baked Alaska to one side and leapt to her feet. "Brava! Brava! This is art! This is true art!! Excellent!!" At 67, Negrescu was the youngest vampire in the café tonight. She was also the only vampire who resembled a movie vamp, as she modeled herself on Theda Bara in *Salome*, all black eyeliner and slave bracelets. Negrescu inherited her beauty and grace from her mother, Viktoriya, a cousin to the Grand Duchess Maria Alexandrovna of Russia. In 1924 Russian nobles were thin on the ground after the Romanovs were thrust into Abraham's bosom by machine-gun fire at Ekaterinburg on July 17th, 1918. "Mr. Karayan, I must ask you, where did you hear that story?"

"I was told the story only a month ago by a vampire visiting from New Orleans. She had once been a pirate. Her name was Mary Read. She impersonated a man and joined the crew on Blackbeard's ship. Fascinating woman. Anyway, she was told the story back in 1845 by Creole in a Red

Turban painted by Jacques Guillaume Lucien Amans, a servant at Manticore House.

Pierre Lemprière-Robin, a French vampire who had once been the lover of King Robert II, the pious and wise, cleared his throat. "I wonder if Creole in a Red Turban painted by Jacques Guillaume Lucien Amans steps back into her own painting and then beyond that into Manticore House. Is that portal between the two worlds still open? I think there's more to this story than meets the eye. It's certainly intriguing. I was surprised 'The Master' was a lettuce. I've never met a lettuce vampire before. I've met a couple of vampire tomatoes, though."

"That surprised me too." Negrescu settled back into her seat. She dipped her fork into the baked Alaska. "I don't know why I was surprised, because thinking about it now, why wouldn't a lettuce be a vampire? Anything or anyone can live forever."

Dario Brone brushed a hair from his Oxford bags, slapped his thighs, stood up, and stepped onto the stage. "With regards to the lettuce, it's not that surprising. In ancient Egypt, the lettuce was not eaten as food but used as an aphrodisiac. The lettuce is a phallic symbol associated with the god of fertility, Min. He is depicted on Egyptian wall paintings with an erect penis, and according to the text from the walls of Edfu Temple, the lettuce helped Min perform the sexual act for days on end. Also, if you break off a lettuce leaf it oozes a white milky substance that looks like sperm. So, to be smitten and bitten by a lettuce is a great honor. But let's move on. Anastazie Miroshnik will tell our next story."

Miroshnik struggled onto the stage carrying a carpetbag, from which she rescued a wad of crumpled papers. The diminutive Miroshnik escaped a Russian pogrom in 1903 after killing a Cossack who attacked her. Andrei Shkuro was a lieutenant in Symon Petliura's Ukrainian People's

Republic Army, responsible for many Russian anti-Jewish pogroms. First, she bit off his penis and spat it out into the snow. While he convulsed, screaming, she split his head open with a shovel, finally strangling him with her bare hands. "Prekratite dushit' menya. Ya ne mogu dyshat." The Cossack pleaded but it was no use, Miroshnik was hellbent on revenge. Dressed as a man, a peasant farmer, she fled her hometown of Kremenchuk, escaping through Poland, then Germany, then across the North Sea to England.

Miroshnik shook out the papers, sending up a cloud of dust into the air. "This story is set in London. It's called *Danse Macabre*."

FOUR

DANSE MACABRE

A Tale Told by Anastazie Miroshnik

London's Highgate Cemetery is a desolate landscape at the best of times, but on March 17, 1883 it was even more so. Karl Marx died three days earlier and though a successful philosopher, less than a dozen teary-eyed Communists wept helplessly into red handkerchiefs at his funeral. The proletariat was either not informed of the event or their invitations were lost in the mail. It was unusually cold for the time of year, the sleet cutting into mourners' faces like icy razors. Black umbrellas, long overcoats, knitted woolen scarves, and gloves, did little to shelter the grieving from the bitter cold. Two years earlier Marx himself stood here at the funeral of his wife, Jenny von Westphalen. The mourners today included Willhelm Liebknecht, a founder of the German Social Democratic Party, two of Marx's daughters, Eleanor and Laura, his sons-in-law Charles Longuet and Paul Lafargue, Communist associates Friedrich Lessner, G. Lochner, Carl Schorlemmer and Ray Lankester, a British zoologist. Also attending was Agatha Dithering-Trubshaw, wife of Geoffrey Dithering-Trubshaw, the Egyptologist. Marx's friend and collaborator, Frederick Engels, read the eulogy, beginning with, "On the 14th of March, at a quarter to three in the afternoon, the greatest living thinker ceased to think. He had been left alone for scarcely two minutes, and when we came back, we found him in his armchair, peacefully gone to sleep—but forever."

Agatha Dithering-Trubshaw shivered. She felt out of place here; her late-husband was the Socialist. She had no political views. Her interests lay elsewhere. Not in overthrowing the ruling class in a violent revolution but in the accumulation of exotic footwear. Her passion was shoes. Geoffrey Dithering-Trubshaw died a month earlier and she was here on a mission. It was his dying wish that if Karl Marx expired before her, Agatha should attend the funeral and bury the Golden Jackal near his grave. Three years earlier, her husband and Swedish Egyptologist Karl Piehl uncovered the tomb of Tuten-Fruitti, the deputy seal-bearer of the Pharaoh King Tuthmosis III (1504 BC-1452 BC), in the city of Luxor, south of Cairo. Dithering-Trubshaw found the gold statuette of Anubis on a shelf in an antechamber, hidden behind a pile of parchment paper scrolls. It was smuggled into Britain and lived in a china cabinet in the Dithering-Trubshaw house in South Kensington. Agatha didn't like it. It gave her the creeps. Rather than being an object with magical, mystical properties, Anubis was just something else for the chambermaid to dust. That said, on her husband's deathbed, Agatha promised she would bury Anubis at Karl Marx's grave. Her husband explained to her: "In the Egyptian Book of the Dead, Anubis is the Golden Jackal Egyptian god. It's the job of Anubis to weigh the hearts of the dead. He weighs them against an ostrich feather. From this he determines the fate of the soul. If the heart is lighter than the feather, then the deceased moves on to a heavenly existence in Duat, the realm of the dead. If the heart is heavier, then the deceased is devoured by Ammit, a female demon, part lion, part hippopotamus, part crocodile." Geoffrey Dithering-Trubshaw wanted nothing more than for Karl Marx to have safe passage into the afterlife.

After Frederick Engels' eulogy, the mourners trickled away until Agatha Dithering-Trubshaw stood alone at the graveside. She looked about her to see if anyone was visiting the graves of loved ones, any prying eyes, Peeping Toms, snoops, spies. For all she knew there was a dark dusty corner of British law that condemned Anubis-buriers to the gallows. She didn't want to swing by her neck on a rope. Agatha Dithering-Trubshaw didn't have time to die. She was busy. She had shoes to buy. Traveling to Highgate Cemetery on a single deck horse-drawn tram, she passed Gabby's Shoe Emporium, where she glimpsed a pair of white leather button boots in the window. As the sleet drummed a loud tattoo on her umbrella, Agatha closed her eyes. She imagined a swarthy sailor kneeling at her feet, kissing those white leather boots and undoing the buttons with his teeth. She purred like a kitten at the thought of it, then whimpered and screamed like a banshee as she shuddered through waves of orgasms. It equaled a 5.8 magnitude earthquake. Rotted corpses rattled underground in their coffins. Rings and bracelets slid off the metacarpals, radii and ulnae of skeletons. Jaws on skulls fell open.

After regaining her composure, Agatha Dithering-Trubshaw laid her umbrella on the grass, took a soup ladle from her handbag, and clawed a hole next to Marx's grave. There she buried Anubis, Guardian of the Scales and Protector of the Dead. As she walked away through the avenues of cold stone angels, crosses, and draped urns, the rain eased up and Ra, the orange spong, in the sky peeked through a gap in the clouds. Praise Ra.

The following day women's hats started disappearing.

Gwendolyn Cartwright visited Highgate Cemetery every Sunday to lay flowers on the grave of her deceased husband.

Richard Cartwright was a distinguished surgeon with a passion for ballet. On May 25, 1870 he attended the premiere of Clément Philibert Léo Delibes' *Coppélia* at the Théâtre Impérial de l'Opéra in Paris. Two days later he unwisely attempted a brisé vole at the top of a staircase. Even at the age of seventy-six he may have survived the fall. That is had he not cracked his head open on an Emperor Kangxi's Qing Dynasty porcelain vase sitting on the landing half way down. That was thirteen years ago, and his wife still visited his grave every Sunday. That was true love. Today, at her husband's gravesite, she felt uneasy, as if she was being watched. She noticed a woodpecker perched on a nearby headstone. It was calling to her, a shrill, high-pitched, hoarse … "tchur … tchur … tchur." It was a warning, but Gwendolyn Cartwright did not speak "woodpecker," so the alarm went unheeded. Anubis shed his gold skin and leapt from his burial place. He was now six feet tall, a muscular creature with the body of a man and the head of a wild dog. Anubis pushed the woman to the ground, tore the hat from her head and ran into a grove of trees and shrubbery. Cartwright screamed bloody murder until two rosy-cheeked policemen arrived.

"Did you see the person who stole your hat?" The first policeman was barely out of school, his face a mass of pimples framing a poorly attempted mustache. The second policeman was rotund and old enough to be his father.

"Yes, I saw him! My hat was stolen by a man with a dog's head." Gwendolyn Cartwright dabbed her eyes with a lace handkerchief.

The investigation began and ended there with the policemen laughing. The hat was recovered later, without the ostrich feathers. Cartwright began to doubt her own sanity. Had she been robbed by a man with a dog's head or not? Or was she following in the footsteps of her Aunt Rosie who was currently gnawing through her leather restraints at St. Mary Bethlehem lunatic asylum?

Anubis now had three ostrich feathers. That night he tore into the grave of Karl Marx, opened the casket, and ripped out the philosopher's heart. The organ seemed small for a man whose ideas were so big. The aorta, pulmonary artery, and the superior vena cava seemed miniscule for the man who wrote that, "Religion is the sigh of the oppressed creature, the heart of a heartless world, just as it is the spirit of a spiritless situation. It is the opium of the people." Anubis held Karl Marx's heart up to the moon and howled, weighing the heart against an ostrich feather from Gwendolyn Cartwright's hat. As Geoffrey Dithering-Trubshaw suspected, Marx's heart was lighter than an ostrich feather. Anubis held two ankhs, one in each hand, across his chest, as he sniffed the air. Drool hung from his lips. He smelt London and its madness – a city permanently teetering on the precipice of chaos. Chaos smells like lawn clippings and fresh sawdust. Anubis replaced the heart and judged Karl Marx worthy of entering Duat.

Anubis continued his work in Highgate Cemetery, weighing the hearts of the dead, sending some souls to paradise, others to be devoured by Ammit. As more Londoners died, more ostrich feathers were needed, and more hats were snatched from the heads of unsuspecting women. By the end of September twenty-five hats were stolen and recovered without their ostrich feathers. The Metropolitan police were at a loss to explain it. The *Pall Mall Gazette* speculated that perhaps the "half dog-man" was an escapee from a traveling freak show. A medical anomaly, like the bearded lady, the lobster-claw boy, Siamese twins, and the girl from Burma afflicted with chin testicles. The news reports grew more and more sensational and it became de rigueur for couples to promenade through Highgate Cemetery hoping for a glimpse of half-dog-man.

The hat snatcher even attracted the attention of notables like Oscar Wilde, who strolled through Highgate Cemetery waving an ostrich feather, accompanied by actress Sarah Bernhardt. Wilde was a green velvet butterfly and "The Divine Sarah" shone brightly, a Parisian star of the Belle Époque. Another couple that came to tempt half-dog-man with an ostrich feather was the Prince of Wales, Albert Edward, and his mistress, Lillie Langtry. None of them saw the half-dog man. Anubis was a sly fox who watched them from the warmth and safety of his shallow grave. He held back. Snatching ostrich feathers from the rich and famous would only bring unwanted attention from the police.

The police searched every inch of Highgate Cemetery but found nothing. Not even half-dog-man droppings. At the end of his tether, Chief Inspector Jonathan Willyfort of the Metropolitan Police devised a devious plan. He ordered police officers, David Johnson and Robert Denslow, to shave off their mutton chop sideburns and pose as widows visiting the graves of deceased husbands. The two policemen donned dresses with floral prints, bustles, wigs with fashionably frizzled fringes, and voluminous hats adorned with ostrich plumes: Johnson wore a chapeau of black straw and Venice lace with a single white ostrich feather and a black veil; Denslow, a blue velvet hat with a burnt orange band and a fountain of ostrich plumes. As the two dressed in the apparel of the opposite sex, only the corsets proved problematic, as both men were broad-shouldered and bearish. Squeezing into the steel-boned hourglass corsets was like sliding marshmallows into keyholes. However, with spade-loads of rouge, powder and lipstick, the two passed as matronly, zaftig, female weightlifters capable of wrestling a stampeding water buffalo to the ground. Johnson and Denslow both carried a muzzle-loading, double-action, percussion Beaumont–Adams revolver in their beaded opera purses along with a powder puff and a bottle of Crabtree and Evelyn Lavender Toilet Water. Half dog-man was as good as dead.

Johnson and Denslow strolled arm-in-arm up Bisham Gardens, then turned right into Swain's Lane and entered the ornate gates of the cemetery.

"And where are you two lovely ladies going to then?" A dapper elderly gentleman wearing a single-breasted morning suit of black worsted, a collarless waistcoat, trousers of black cashmere, black leather shoes, and white button-down spats, balanced precariously on a gold-topped cane. "How would you like to come to my house for some excitement? There will, of course, be a financial remuneration. All I ask is that you stand astride me and pass water upon my nether regions."

"No thank you, we're not that kind of girls." Johnson stared at the ground briefly, then moved on.

The elderly gentleman grasped Johnson's arm. "Now that's no way to treat a gentleman who offers only kindness and companionship."

Johnson pulled away. "And that's no way to treat a lady. Is it, Marjorie?"

"No, it's not, Emily." Denslow removed his black satin elbow gloves, bloodied the gentlemen's nose, kicked him between the legs and toppled him onto the path. After checking to see who was around, the two "ladies" lifted their skirts and urinated on the prostrate predator who had passed out cold.

Marjorie and Emily, the two "ladies" promenaded for an hour shaded by their parasols. Anubis saw the female impersonators but wisely left them alone. Snatching hats from two policemen wearing blue ribbon bow corsets and black leather ankle boots could prove counterproductive. Three days later Anubis snatched another hat. This one from Mary Quatrain, a widow whose husband had been a hot-air balloonist – before a storm blew him out to sea and his body washed up on the Brittany coast a week later. Throughout September and October more hats were snatched, more hearts weighed, and more souls dispatched into the afterlife, or into the jaws of Ammit. In the end the police gave up and moved on to more pressing crimes like murder, rape, and hungry street urchins stealing bread.

On October 31st the undead celebrated Samhain in Highgate Cemetery with a Vampire Costume Ball. As midnight approached, a caravan of horse-drawn hearses drove through the gates. The first to arrive was Fleurdelice Gabor, Queen of the gypsy vampires. The coachman opened the back door, revealing a double-coffin inside. Gabor climbed out the casket dressed in her most exquisite ball gown of dark blue shimmering velvet and white lace. Across her eyes she wore a Venetian filigree metal mask encrusted with sapphires and rubies. Gabor took a folded lace handkerchief from her purse, shook it out and blotted a pearl of blood at the corner of her lips. Her lover, Luca Giordano, lay comatose in the coffin, his bloodied privates exposed. Away from prying eyes, behind the purple drapery covering the windows of the hearse, Gabor gorged upon Giordano's cock throughout the journey from Belladonna, her Knightsbridge mansion. She slid his cock into her mouth, bit down with her fangs and sucked the "fear of death" out of him. Giordano was now smitten and bitten, a freshly turned vampire. Gabor smiled, leaned back into the hearse and touched his face. "You were delicious. You taste of milk and honey."

More hearses and carriages arrived. Some undead came on foot, bedraggled in rags. Others appeared in puffs of smoke or flew in on bat wings, magic carpets, and straddling dragons. Several hundred vampires, zombies, restless ghosts, poltergeists, shadow people, draugr and Chinese jiangshi, gathered around the gravestones in Highgate Cemetery. Some embraced old friends, while others stood alone, pensive, brooding, vacant. Under the moonlight, vampire nuns from Our Lady of the Dead Brides of Christ convent passed through the crowd like long-forgotten memories, conundrums, or unanswered questions. The undead throng fell silent when a middle-aged bearded gentleman arrived. He was magnificent. He was a prince. He was a princess. He was a king. He was a queen. He wore a black frockcoat, high waisted pants, a dress shirt, vest, cravat, top hat, boots, gloves, spats, and a pocket watch. It was the honored guest, Camille Saint-Saëns, the French composer. The crowd applauded his arrival. Some bowed their heads out of respect. A halo of moths fluttered around his head, attracted by the sweet nectar and glow of his genius. Behind his carriage walked the musicians of L'Orchestre des Vampires euphoriques carrying their instruments: a piccolo, two flutes, two oboes, two clarinets, two bassoons, four horns, two trumpets, three trombones, one tuba, a percussion section including timpani, xylophone, bass drum, cymbals and triangle, and a harp and strings.

Anubis hid in a grove of trees. He flexed his muscles nervously and wiped drool from his lips with his arm. He shivered in the nighttime chill. Anubis rightfully feared the undead. The whole purpose of his existence was to guide humans into the afterlife or toss them into the jaws of Ammit. Vampires were the antithesis of everything Anubis stood for. To vampires, the Golden Jackal was a mischief-maker, an irritant, a floundering fly in their canopic jars of scented ointment. They were immortal enemies.

Anubis crouched low in the undergrowth, his nose twitching nervously. He watched Saint-Saëns clamber up Karl Marx's tombstone and perch on the top. Before him the orchestra set up on a gravel path, some standing, others leaning against gravestones. As two vampires approached, Anubis crouched lower in the undergrowth. One of them, James Frogmorten, worked in Spitalfields fruit and vegetable market. Jack Dunsany, the other, was an author. Dunsany tugged at the brim of his homburg hat. "Good evening to you. I have never been to this Ball before. What happens here?" The author inhaled from his cigarette and blew smoky rings into the damp night air.

"Every year London's undead come here to dance for Death. We dance until dawn and the emergence of Ra, the orange spong." Frogmorten smiled.

"So where is Death?"

"There, atop the tombstone of Karl Marx, with the violin." Frogmorten pointed at Saint-Saëns, as the composer lifted the violin and began to stamp a beat with his heel on the tombstone. L'Orchestre des Vampires euphoriques began to play Saint-Saëns' own composition, *Danse Macabre* inspired by a Henri Cazalis poem: *Zig, zig, zig, Death in cadence, Striking a tomb with his heel, Death at midnight plays a dance-tune, Zig, zig, zag, on his violin.*

The following morning, when Ra, the orange spong, peered over the horizon and spat beams of light onto Highgate Cemetery, the undead were gone. There was no trace of a Vampire Ball ever having taken place. All was quiet and peaceful again. A goldfinch perched on a gravestone, singing a short and dry descending trill. A flock of geese flew overhead, honking as if gasping for breath. The gates of Highgate Cemetery creaked open as Agatha Dithering-Trubshaw entered for the second and last time. She was there to complete the pledge she made to her husband. It was a delicate autumn day, a carpet of wet fallen leaves on the ground. As she approached Karl Marx's grave, Dithering-Trubshaw stopped to admire the quietude. She inhaled deeply. She could smell the roses left on the grave of Martha Hogsflesh, a woman "taken from us while too young, leaving baby Victoria a motherless child."

A seagull, flying overhead, pooped a stream of chalky-white slime onto Dithering-Trubshaw's dress. "Oh no!" She dabbed the mess with a handkerchief, unpinned a white gardenia corsage from her lapel, and moved it to cover the stain.

At Karl Marx's gravesite she dug up Anubis with the soup ladle, brushed off the soil and wrapped him in a black silk scarf. She then took a carriage to the Lyceum Theatre at 21 Wellington Street. The current production was *Ingomar* by Henry E. Abbey, starring the Victorian stage actor Henry Irving. At the box office she asked a matronly ticket-seller for the theater's business manager. After a minute or so a handsome, bearded man appeared. "Can I help you Madam?" His Irish brogue was thick as treacle.

"I believe this belongs to you."

"What is it?"

"It's a gold statuette of the Egyptian God Anubis."

Agatha Dithering Trubshaw handed him the gold statuette, turned and walked away.

"At least tell me your name." The man called out to her.

The woman stopped and turned. "My name is Agatha Dithering-Trubshaw. You don't know me. You don't need to know me."

"Aren't you going to ask my name?"

Dithering-Trubshaw continued walking. She was in a hurry. On the way there she passed a shoe store where she saw a pair of delightful red silk evening slippers in the window. She had to have them.

Bram Stoker cupped Anubis in the palm of his hand and muttered under his breath. "What am I supposed to do with this?"

FIVE

BACK AT THE VAMP-ART CAFÉ

The patrons of the Vamp-Art Café leapt to their feet, clapped and cheered uproariously. "Brava! Brava!" The walls shook slightly, teacups rattled in their saucers, jewelry jingled, a sherry trifle on the countertop wobbled, and Dario Brone fanned himself with a menu. Anastazie Miroshnik smiled and bowed low from the waist. She loved telling stories. Her heart, though cold as ice cream and as dead as a doornail, still fluttered. *Danse Macabre* was her favorite vampire story. Anubis appeared in many vampire tales, as the Golden Jackal was also a child of Ra, the orange spong. Ra sent Anubis out of the Garden of Eden to guide mortals into the afterlife or hell, but that was before mortals began destroying the planet, beginning with the industrial revolution. That's another story. A story we know only too well.

"Is that true about Bram Stoker? Did he really work at the Lyceum Theatre in London? It seems unlikely." Jenny O'Brien, an Irish vampire, bared her fangs and hissed as she spit out the words.

"Oh yes, it's true." Miroshnik nodded. "Stoker worked at the theater for many years. Some say he was the lover of the actor, Henry Irving."

Margaret Hall, a stout vampire wearing a cummerbund, monocle, green carnation, spats, and tails, rose to her feet. "And Bram Stoker's wife, Florence, was once engaged to Oscar Wilde. It seems she was drawn to 'temperamental' men. Men of the Uranian persuasion." Hall was formidable, built like an outside privy, sturdy as the First National Bank of Chicago. Chrysanthemums wilted under her disapproving glare – she did not like flowers. Opium poppies inhaled and overdosed in her presence. It was said she could bring a train to a shuddering halt just by glancing at it. Though it was also said, she was a kindly soul, especially to former and current lovers. "There's one thing I don't understand," Hall continued. "At the end of the story Bram Stoker held Anubis and asked, 'What am I supposed to do with this?' I'm wondering what he did with it. *Dracula* was published many years later. Do you think Anubis played a part in Stoker writing that book? Anubis fears the undead because we undermine his life's mission, to guide souls to the other side. At the very least, Anubis might have influenced the author, but how? Perhaps he fed Stoker scurrilous lies about vampires. Maybe Anubis himself wrote that terrible book, and Stoker merely transcribed it. Could Stoker be the innocent party in all this? Perhaps *Dracula* was written by Anubis. It makes sense when you think about it."

A tsunami of skepticism flooded the Vamp-Art Café, washing away any nascent sympathy for the author of *Dracula*. Miroshnik shrugged. "Sadly, we can't ask Mr. Stoker as he is long passed away, his ashes now on display at Golders Green Crematorium. The real question is, 'Where is Anubis now?' I'd certainly like to know!"

Edelweiss von Trapp, a strikingly handsome woman, mysterious as a magician's card trick, wearing flowing Bohemian silks and dainty Chinese slippers, leapt to her feet. "I don't think we'll ever know the answer to that question. Anubis is famously elusive. Even Ra, the orange spong, can't find him. *Danse Macabre* was a thrilling story, though. A rattling good yarn." Von Trapp danced around the tables in the Vamp-Art Café like a fairy with her wings on fire, silk scarves dangling from her wrists. She was a veteran of Isadora Duncan's School of Dance in Berlin-Grunewald, Germany, a member of the Isadorables dance troop. While touring, von Trapp became the lover of Glykeria Stavros, the oldest vampire lesbian in Greece, a friend of the poet Sappho. Stavros had smitten and bitten von Trapp after she danced at the Athenian Acropolis in the ruins of the Theatre of Dionysus Eleuthereus. She drained von Trapp of her "fear of death." She gifted her with immortality, a manifesto, an agenda, and a mission. To save the planet from selfish mortals.

Giorgio Graffelley banged his fist on a table. "It matters not what Anubis contributed to that book. Its evil intent is clear. I would like to read you something I recently found. This is the *Chicago Tribune* review of *Dracula* dated November 30, 1899. It begins: 'If Bram Stoker has any time to spare from his duties as Henry Irving's business manager it would be well for him to devote it to some more harmless recreation than that of creating literary vampires. This is said after reading his *Dracula,* published by Doubleday & McClure. There are but two things of interest about the book. One is a sense of wonder that any normal mind could conceive of ideas so loathsome, and the other that anyone could get it printed. It is about a human vampire who lives on human blood, and the story, which is in the form of a journal, relates, with exhaustive and sickening details, the monster's habits and ways and means of satisfying his appetite. An opposing power of light for the hideous thing of darkness might have given the story a redeeming trait, but there is none.'"

"An accurate review of an inaccurate book." Von Trapp conceded. "Blood-sucking vampires do not exist, only in fiction. We bite, we puncture the skin, we taste blood, thereby releasing the pent-up, soul-destroying fear of death. We then gift immortality. The review is correct, Bram Stoker's Dracula is a monster. He feeds on innocents, whereas we offer immortality."

A pall of silence fell upon the vampires in the Vamp-Art Café. Miroshnik returned to her seat.

Dario Brone brushed back his unruly mop of black curls and stepped onto the stage. "Thank you Anastazie Miroshnik for that excellent story. Our next storyteller is British-born Samuel Smyth-Robinson."

Immaculately dressed in a worsted suit, Smyth-Robinson sported a cropped beard and neat mustache waxed at the tips. He was a handsome man with an equally handsome lover. He and Richard Quartermaine had been together for over 300 years. Like all vampires, Smyth-Robinson often reinvented himself, out of necessity. When you are immortal, you are forced to change your identity often. Usually, before your lack of ageing is noticed. This often involves disappearing entirely, or moving to a new town, or country, severing ties with friends and family. Before the Great "1914-1918" War, Smyth-Robinson was a teacher at the prestigious Rugby School, teaching Greek and Latin to ungrateful pubescent boys. He taught there for three years, then changed his identity and moved on. At various times he was James Biggerstaff, Robert Candida, Maurice Clapperton, and briefly, Sebastian Binky-Raffles. Smyth-Robinson and Quartermaine moved to Chicago in 1918, years after the publication of Bram Stoker's *Dracula*. "We came late to the party" is what he told friends. Currently, Smyth-Robinson and Quartermaine ran Pixies and Petals, a flower shop, in Towertown, a few doors away from the Vamp-Art Café.

Smyth-Robinson cleared his throat and wiped his brow with a tussah silk handkerchief. "My story is a tale of three sister-vampires, Emily, Anne and Charlotte Bronte. It's called *Three Sisters in Exile*. There is nothing unusual about this story, nothing that will surprise you. As vampires in exile we all have a similar story to tell. This is a typical story of the vampire diaspora to America after the publication of Bram Stoker's *Dracula*."

SIX

THREE SISTERS IN EXILE

A Tale Told by Samuel Smyth-Robinson

The three sisters tugged their shawls about their shoulders as they shivered in St. Michael and All Angels' Church in Haworth, Yorkshire. It was a cold winter morning in December 1899. Outside, sheets of icy rain cut into the blustery wind, doubling the misery of the inhabitants of this small northern English town. On these bleak Yorkshire Moors there was little to block the weather from its trajectory, its natural course. Yet, it was here in this windswept landscape that great novels were written. Stories still read today.

The town of Haworth stands near the Pennine Way, a 267-mile trail down the middle of England. It's often called "the backbone of Britain." The area around Haworth is known for its waterfalls and is a natural habitat for otters, deer, and golden plovers. Charlotte Bronte once described the waterfalls as, *Fine indeed; a perfect torrent racing over the rocks, white and beautiful.* The Bronte sisters and their books had long since merged into these Yorkshire Moors. They were one. Inseparable.

In St. Michael and All Angels' Church, the three sisters stood before the family tomb. The inscription read:

THE BRONTE FAMILY VAULT IS SITUATED BELOW THIS PILLAR, NEAR TO THE PLACE WHERE THE BRONTE'S PEW STOOD IN THE OLD CHURCH. THE FOLLOWING MEMBERS OF THE FAMILY WERE BURIED HERE. MARIA AND PATRICK, MARIA, ELIZABETH, BRANWELL, EMILY JANE, CHARLOTTE.

The only Bronte family member not listed on the tomb was Anne. She read the inscription twice and stamped her feet to keep warm. "It's bitter cold here. That's why I was buried in St. Mary's churchyard in Scarborough. I didn't want to be buried here in this wretched place. I wanted to be close to the raging North Sea, taste the salt, lay witness to the tides. I wanted to be buried near where I picked up shells and tiptoed barefoot amidst the seaweed and driftwood. I 'died' May 28, 1849 and was revived and born again as a vampire the following day."

"I 'died' December 19, 1848." Emily draped her shawl across her head and tied it under her chin. "I was also revived and born again as a vampire the following day."

"And I 'died' March 31, 1855." Charlotte smiled. "I remember the day well. I was the last of our father's children to die. I was revived and born again as a vampire the night I was buried."

Of course, Anne, Emily and Charlotte Bronte weren't dead at all. They were undead. The three sisters were smitten, bitten, and given a sleeping draft on their deathbeds by farmer Geoffrey Giles, a grizzled vampire with a heart of gold. Giles lived alone at Clappit Farm, tended his sheep, chickens, and cows, and was an admirer of the Bronte sisters' books. Emily's *Wuthering Heights*, Charlotte's *Jane Eyre*, and Anne's *The Tenant of Wildfell Hall* were favorites. He read them over and over, absorbing every word, bathing in the romance, drama, and tragedy leaping from the pages. Giles knew the sisters' father, the Rev. Patrick Bronte, and attended dinner parties at the Haworth parsonage. He also befriended their brother, Branwell, and had tried to save him from his drunkenness and opium addiction. In that, he failed. In saving the sisters, he succeeded.

As each of the sisters lay dying, their bodies racked by consumption, Giles drained them of the "fear of death." For mortals, death is an end, a cause for fear. As the fear collectively builds up, it creates a layer of pent-up poisonous gas on planet Earth. By piercing the Bronte sisters, Giles used global acupuncture to release that gas and diffuse the tension. Giles couldn't allow the Bronte sisters' talent to die, their pens to be discarded, or the rushing river of words dry up. And so, one by one, he released them from the pressure of mortality and gifted them with eternal life. Emily first, followed by Anne, finally Charlotte. With each of the dying sisters, Giles was there with kind words, holding their hands. He was there at each of the funerals, two in Haworth, one in Scarborough, officiated by their father, Rev. Patrick Bronte.

At each of the services, Rev. Bronte said:

Depart, Christian soul, from this world, in the name of God the Father almighty who created you; in the name of Jesus Christ, Son of the living God, who suffered for you; in the name of the Holy Spirit who sanctified you; in the name of the glorious and blessed Virgin Mary, Mother of God; in the name of St. Joseph, her illustrious spouse; in the name of the Angels and Archangels, Thrones and Dominations, Principalities and Powers, Cherubim and Seraphim; in the name of the patriarchs and prophets, the holy apostles and evangelists, the holy martyrs and confessors, the holy monks and hermits; in the name of the holy virgins and all the holy men and women of God. May you rest in peace this day and your abode be in holy Sion; through Christ our Lord. Amen.

After each funeral, Giles returned later to open their coffins and revive the sisters from their drugged slumbers. Nobody suspected the Bronte sisters' graves were disturbed. For decades their admirers left red roses and notes at their empty gravesites without a hint of suspicion. After robbing the graves, Giles smuggled each of the revived sisters south to London. There they lived in Russell Square in a commune with other undead artists and poets. The sisters continued writing under nom de plumes: Emily (Suzanne Smothers) wrote articles and stories for *The Strand*, Anne (Katherine Theroux) reviewed books for T*he Bookman*, and Charlotte (Sarah Johnson) contributed to *The Ludgate Monthly*. Under other names they also wrote novels, plays, and poetry.

Now, on December 31, 1899, the fin de siècle, the three sisters returned to Haworth for the first time since their un-deaths. As children, it was here on these desolate moors they ran wild as brown hares and Shetland ponies. They picked reeds and wove them into riding crops. Bunches of heather were used as a medicinal tea for kidney, prostate enlargement, fluid retention, gout, arthritis, sleep disorders, breathing problems, cough, and colds. Nothing could harness the free spirit of the Bronte sisters. Now, they were back in Haworth to visit the cave under Penistone Crag, the outcrag of gritstone rock where Cathy romanced Heathcliff in *Wuthering Heights*. Although fictionalized in a novel, it was indeed a real place.

However this story makes no sense unless we peel back the years, to when the Bronte sisters were young and carried the wind in their hair. One morning in June 1830, nine years after their mother died from ovarian cancer, Emily ran past her father, the Rev. Patrick Bronte, out the door of their parsonage home, and across the moors to Penistone Crag. She was followed by Anne and Charlotte, neither as agile as their sister. Emily was Hermes, son of Zeus, wearing talaria on her feet, flying with ease between the worlds of the mortal and divine. Compared to celestial Emily, the other two sisters were mere mortals tagging along behind. At the Crag, Emily sat on a rock, caught her breath and opened the recently published *Our Village: Sketches of Rural Character and Scenery* by Mary Russell Mitford. She read:

... defiance of wet and cold, grumble at the warmth and dryness of his apartment. He used to foretell that it would kill him, and assuredly it did so. Never could the typhus fever have found out that wild hillside, or have lurked under that broken roof."

Emily rested the book in her lap, closed her eyes and pondered the words. Nearby, Charlotte and Anne tossed a ball back and forth, repeating rhymes:

One, two, three O'Leary
four, five, six O'Leary
seven, eight, nine O'Leary
Ten O'Leary
Catch the ball."

Or:

A sailor went to sea sea sea
to see what he could see see see
but all that he could see see see
was the bottom of the deep blue sea sea sea

Charlotte bounced the ball off a rock. It ricocheted twice then disappeared. "Oh no, I fear it is lost." Charlotte stamped her foot and searched for the ball in a patch of golden saxifrage.

"It went in there!" Anne pointed to a cleft between two large boulders. "It's dark. I think it's a cave."

Charlotte clambered up the rocks and squeezed through the crevice, while Emily and Anne waited outside.

"Have you found it?" Anne called out after a full minute. There was no answer. She called again.

"Come inside." Charlotte's voice was faint, as if rising-up from a deep lichen-covered well in a Grimms' fairy tale. "You must see this."

Anne and Emily lifted their skirts and petticoats and squeezed through the crevice. It opened into a damp, dark cave. From the sliver of light beaming through the crack they saw stalactites hanging from the roof and stalagmites rising up from the floor to meet them. Through the center of the cave, a babbling stream trickled along a gulley in the hard rock floor it carved for itself over centuries.

"It's Gondal!" Charlotte laughed and clapped her hands. "It really exists."

Gondal was an imaginary world created by Emily and Anne and featured in their juvenile writings. It was an island in the North Pacific, a land of gallantry, manners and adventure. Gondal included at least four kingdoms: Gondal, Angora, Exina and Alcona. In a poem, Emily wrote:

But thou art now on the desolate sea,
thinking of Gondal and grieving for me;
Longing to be in sweet Elbe again,
Thinking and grieving and longing in vain.

Emily's eyes lit up. "Yes, I believe this is Gondal. What do you think Anne?"

"I think you're right." Anne began to cry. "I thought we imagined it but here it is. Gondal is a real place. It was just waiting here all the time, waiting for us to find it. It proves what I have long thought, that imagining something for long enough makes it real."

"I wonder how far back the cave goes. It's too dark to see. We must return tomorrow with candles." Charlotte guided her sisters out of the cave like a mallard herding her ducklings. As the eldest daughter, she assumed her deceased mother's mantle. Their father, though a pious and religious man, was ill-equipped for parenting. He was adept at guiding his flock into heaven, but his own children were left to their own devices. To run wild on those desolate Yorkshire Moors.

The following day the sisters returned to Penistone Crag with a picnic basket, a candlestick and candles, and a box of sulfur-tipped matches. Again, they squeezed through the crevice into the dark cave. Emily lit the candles and with each flame, more of the cave's secrets were revealed. Carrying the candlestick, Charlotte led the way deeper into Gondal. They clambered down a steep rocky slope, through a narrow chamber leading to a cavernous hall and a vast subterranean lake. Here they laid out a picnic blanket on the hard rock floor and helped themselves to cucumber sandwiches, cheese, and stone jars of ginger ale. They talked of Gondal and the adventures that took place there. Of men of honor and women of virtue.

"I wonder where the inhabitants of Gondal went? Nobody lives here now." Emily bit into an apple.

Anne brushed a ringlet of hair from her face. "I think they sailed away across this lake. They are most likely fishing, or perhaps there is some intrigue taking place in a far-off land. I'm sure that soon their ships will return, and we will be told stories of their adventures."

Charlotte lifted the candlestick and peered out across the lake. "I can't see the other side. The lake goes on for miles."

"Hundreds of miles." Anne giggled.

The three sisters visited Gondal, their secret world under Penistone Crag, often after that. When Emily "died," the remaining two sisters regularly visited the magical cave. After Anne was gone, Charlotte went there alone. However, after Charlotte "died," nobody visited the secret cave. It remained empty apart from the Bronte sisters' stories of Gondal floating in the air like dandelion seeds on a stiff breeze. Over the years, in their London apartments in Russell Square, they often spoke of Gondal and the happy times they spent there. Even as they matured as vampires, the sisters kept a childlike sense of wonderment.

So why were the Bronte sisters returning to Penistone Crag now, at the fin de siècle? It was a question only a mortal would ask. Over two years earlier, on May 26, 1897, Bram Stoker's *Dracula* was published. The book misrepresented vampires and cast them in a negative light. In the book, Dracula says: "There is no life in this body. I am nothing, lifeless, soulless, hated and feared. I am dead to all the world – hear me! I am the monster that breathing men would kill. I am Dracula."

Vampires are not lifeless and soulless. Vampires are not monsters. Vampires do not sleep in coffins. And far from fearing the sun, vampires worship Ra, the orange spong, in the sky. After all, Ra, the orange spong, created vampires at the dawn of time. Some vampires work in offices during the day, or they till the land on farms, or are machinists in William Blake's dark satanic mills, or they are policemen or florists or milliners. Some vampires are not human. Yes, some are sideboards, geraniums, or buttons on jackets. Vampires are everywhere. The publication of *Dracula* sent a chill down the spines of vampires like Emily, Anne and

Charlotte Bronte. They feared a persecution and made plans to flee England for America.

At Penistone Crag the sisters entered the dank cave for the last time. As they did when they were children, they danced amongst the stalactites and stalagmites, those majestic calcium salts deposited by dripping water. Emily insisted they were the upside-down and down-side up cathedrals of Gondal. Then the three sisters made their way through the tunnels until they reached the banks of the subterranean lake. There they sat and told stories, recited poetry, laughed, and cried with sadness and joy over memories of their childhood. At midnight, a cold wind passed through the cavern and the sisters stood up, formed a circle and held hands. The sisters detected a sweet smell in the air, jasmine and a hint of chaos. They shuddered like the tortured victims of St. Vitus Dance, screamed like banshees, then cracked like eggs tapped on the rim of a glass bowl. The three broken sister-eggs shifted shape to become peregrine hawks. Their backs and wings a bluish-black, underparts white with bands of rusty brown, long narrow tails black with a white tip. The three hawks circled the cave, flew out through the crevice in the rock, then across the countryside. They flew southwest over Rochdale and Manchester until they reached the Liverpool docks on the Mersey River, a center for Shipping and Commerce. There the ships imported and exported produce from countries around the world: from China, the jungles of the Amazon, the plains of India, grain from the banks of the St. Lawrence River, olives from Italy. The sister-hawks found Victoria Dock and perched on the crow's nest atop the mast of the RMS Campania, a British ocean liner owned by the Cunard Steamship Line Shipping Company.

Six days later the stowaways saw the Statue of Liberty, the Manhattan Skyline, and the Ellis Island Immigrant Station. From their perch high above, they watched the bedraggled passengers disembark, carrying their meager belongings on their back, looking like weary snails. The three sister-hawks heard chattering in different languages and saw the fear and excitement on immigrant faces. Then at nightfall the hawks flew through the dark cavernous streets of New York City to Greenwich Village.

In 1900 Greenwich Village was on the cusp of the Gilded Age and the emergence of Bohemia. A time when the "fashionable set" migrated northward to Fifth Avenue and Central Park and artists, writers and radicals moved in. The Village had already inspired Henry James' books *Washington Square* and *The Age of Innocence.* The three sisters were welcomed into La Maison Des Morts-Vivants, a commune of vampire artists, painters, dancers and writers. There, under new names, they published poems and short stories on Donald Evans' Claire Marie Press at 3 East 14th St. They met other writers, like Jack London, Upton Sinclair, Mark Twain, and Mary Heaton Vorse. They also met a young Eugene O'Neill at the Hell Hole, a seedy Irish bar at the corner of 6th and 4th St., also frequented by actors and writers from the Provincetown Playhouse nearby.

The three sisters lived in Greenwich Village for two years, then reinvented themselves and moved back to England. That's where the three Bronte sisters appeared in a film adaptation of *Wuthering Heights*, directed by Albert Victor Bramble. Emily played Cathy under the name Ann Trevor, Charlotte played Mrs. Linton under the name Dora De Winton, and Anne played Catherine under the name Colette Brettel. How do I know this? Because I, Samuel Smyth-Robinson, played the role of Heathcliff under the name Milton Rosmer.

SEVEN

BACK AT THE VAMP-ART CAFÉ

Samuel Smyth-Robinson bowed and soaked up the applause like a smug sea sponge. Annie Farthing stood up. "Thank you for telling us the story. I was unaware the Bronte sisters were members of our vampire family. I shall look at their books with renewed interest."

"I knew their mother." Geoffrey Smallwood, a diminutive vampire with a black pork pie hat and a Fu-Manchu mustache, sat upright in his seat. "Yes, I knew the Bronte sisters' mother, Maria Branwell, before she married Patrick Bronte. She lived in Penzance, the very south coast of England. It must have been around 1810. I also knew Maria's father, Thomas, rather wealthy, a merchant who owned several properties. Maria was seventeen then and quite shy. Wrote poetry, I remember that. Nobody could have guessed she would give birth to three of the finest authors the world has seen."

Jebediah Frost, a dwarfish vampire, raked his fingers through his long straggly graying beard. "Now we know that Emily Bronte is a vampire; the relationship between Cathy and Heathcliff in Wuthering Heights has new meaning."

Smyth-Robinson stiffened, puffed out his chest like a cornered adder. "But Wuthering Heights was written before

Emily Bronte was a vampire. Therefore, presumably, the story was devoid of any vampire-influence." His nostrils flared like a beaten-down shire horse. There was nothing Smyth-Robinson liked more than belittling others. Only by making others small could he feel big.

"Of course, I apologize. I was not thinking." Frost bared his fangs and shrank into his seat.

Several audience members had things to say but feared chastisement by the arrogant Smyth-Robinson. He was not popular in undead circles. He thought because he had performed anal sex on Anna Pavlova, the wife of King William II of the Netherlands, that he was better than everyone else. After scanning the blank faces in the audience, Smyth-Robinson left the stage and returned to his seat next to Richard Quartermaine, his long-suffering lover. Quartermaine stopped listening to Smyth-Robinson two years into their 300-year relationship. One day, he had simply heard enough and shut down. Though strikingly handsome, Quartermaine's demeanor and vacant visage were closer to that of a zombie than a vampire. In Smyth-Robinson's absence, Quartermaine could be amusing and erudite, but as soon as Smyth-Robinson returned his face dropped as if struck by palsy. They were an odd couple.

Dario Brone returned to the stage. "Our next storyteller needs no introductions, because who does not know Lucine Runesque-López, the oldest vampire in the room? Please welcome her."

The patter of polite applause fluttered about the Vamp-Art Café like butterflies feeding on a buddleia bush on a hot summer's afternoon. Runesque-López may be the oldest vampire in the room but she looked eighteen with her Mary Pickford golden curls, silk crepe de Chine dress and slave bracelets. When Julius Caesar ruled the Roman Empire, she had been smitten and bitten by a Vestal Virgin at the Temple of Vesta. Runesque-López has had many guises over the years, most often as a nun. For many years she was the Abbess at the Convent of St. John of Jerusalem in Nottingham in England before masquerading as a man in renaissance Italy, Giusto Barbamachollo, a Venetian merchant. Her latest incarnation was as an artist, dabbling in surrealism. Her current piece, a painting of four spoons nailed to a blue elephant, was called "Removing Marie Antoinette's Other Artichoke Without Closing the Larder Door." The picture was to be nailed to the head of a dead pig and viewed through a keyhole.

"My story is called The Other Side of 'The Door.'" Runesque-López opened a sheaf of papers and began reading.

EIGHT

THE OTHER SIDE OF 'THE DOOR'

A Tale Told by Lucine Runesque-López

Bubbles LaGrasse, born Betty Griswold, was a typical London theatrical boarding house landlady: middle-aged, a spinster – though not without suitors – judgmental, and surviving on a steady diet of gossip and intrigue. She ran the Newberry boarding house in St. Martin's Lane in London's Covent Garden. Not a salubrious neighborhood in 1905. The crowded streets were teeming with barkers, newsboys, organ grinders, women of easy virtue, and child-pickpockets. LaGrasse described it as "a cultural desert inhabited by two-legged scorpions and poisonous snakes."

LaGrasse was a large woman who patted her hair a lot. The mountainous bird nest, balanced atop her head, suffered badly from slippage. In a strong wind her hair capsized altogether, leaving her adrift in a sea of embarrassment. Also, though it may seem unkind to mention it, LaGrasse was in no danger of winning a beauty contest, even if she were the only contestant. That didn't stop her dressing like a street tart, hell-bent on displaying her cleavage to the world, whether the world wanted to see it or not. Her exceptional bosom was the icing on a rather bland fruit cake. One boarder, a Music Hall comic, suggested her breasts were large enough to suckle a litter of pigs. Another wag suggested they resembled two pigs wrestling in a flour sack.

To prospective tenants LaGrasse parroted the same line: "I run a clean establishment here. There will be no visitors of the opposite sex. No canoodling. I'm a woman of the world but I don't want goings-on going-on here at the Newberry. Here's a key to your room but no key to the front door, which I lock at midnight. If you're not back by midnight you can sleep near the dustbins in the alley at the back." This was said with a scowl on her face and fat arms folded across her chest like redwood tree roots.

The Newberry stood four stories high with a poet's garret at the top. The garret was currently rented to "The Great Corum," a ventriloquist performing in a variety show at the Canterbury Music Hall on Westminster Bridge Road, Lambeth. Also on the bill were Bobo and Bunky, two Rumanian acrobats; Billie Wells, a female impersonator with a recurring skin problem; comedian Champagne Charlie; Percy Val, the tipsy tumbler; singing trio, the Fawcett sisters; and twins Jeff and Jenny Trip with Flip, their performing poodle. After rumors of incest, the aforementioned Music Hall comic suggested the twins were Siamese twins "joined at the privates." Their abiding affection for each other fueled speculation and gossip about their "exotic" love life. Their deep-love for Flip, the poodle, served only to spice up the tittle-tattle. Canoodling and poodling indeed.

It was seven o'clock in the morning when Bubbles La Grasse banged on the door to the garret. Inside, a beam of sunlight pierced the dormer window in the one room attic. Two writhing figures on the bed froze in a pornographic tableau vivant. Squirrels scurried across the roof seeking cover under the eaves, their peace and privacy shattered. Pigeons reluctantly fled the guttering.

"(Bang-Bang-Bang!) Stop that racket! I know what you're up to. I wasn't born yesterday. (Bang-Bang-Bang!)" The noise woke everyone in the house. "Open this door now!"

"We're just rehearsing, Miss LaGrasse." The Great Corum struggled to calm his panting breath.

"Rehearsing what? That's what I'd like to know. It sounds like you're rehearsing a French postcard in there."

The Great Corum slipped into a pair of trousers and a shirt, then opened the door. "Come in." He gestured with a dramatic sweep of his arm. "You are very welcome."

La Grasse brushed past him. "I know there's a woman in here." She peered under the bed and huffed with disappointment. There was nobody else in the room, except for Jerry Fisher, the ventriloquist's doll, lying face down on the bed with his checkered trousers down around his ankles.

"I was sure I could hear someone else in this room. There were noises of a disgusting nature. Fornicating noises."

"As you can see, there's nobody here." The Great Corum feigned hurt and indignation. He could milk this. "I can't understand why you think so badly of me. I have always been home before midnight. My rent is always paid on time. I abide by the rules of the house. Yet you accuse me of fornication."

"Well, I apologize." LaGrasse scanned the room one last time. She could smell a rat, but no rat could be found. She was livid.

After LaGrasse's shamefaced exit, The Great Corum returned to the matter in hand. Jerry Fisher gasped and stifled a scream as the ventriloquist entered him.

"Fuck me, fuck me hard."

"How hard, Mr. Fisher?"

"As hard as Chinese arithmetic."

For a ventriloquist's doll, Jerry Fisher's language was shocking, certainly unsuited to the polite tea and crumpets world of Edwardian society. His previous owner, Jim C. Vincent, was a merchant seaman, a foul-mouthed Jolly Jack Tar. With him, Jerry Fisher sailed the seven seas. He once docked in Shanghai on the Kwangtung, a steamship of the China Navigation Company, returning to England carrying spices and illicit opium. He once rounded the Cape of Good Hope in Africa, sailed through the Suez Canal to Constantinople and the Black Sea, also to the Americas, north and south. On those adventures, Jerry Fisher entertained seafaring men with his witty banter. Not just his banter, for many sailor's strutting cocks crowed inside of him, unloaded seamen semen in that moist garden between his wooden ass cheeks.

Passion sated, Jerry Fisher lit a State Express cigarette and rested his head on the pillow. He blew smoke rings into the air. They crashed into the ceiling. The Great Corum propped the doll up in a chair. "I've told you a million times not to smoke in bed. It's dangerous. We'd better get ready for breakfast."

"Why do I have to come with you? I don't eat anything. It's one of the perks of being wooden. May I remind you of *The Adventures of Pinocchio* by Carlo Collodi, about a wooden puppet … "

" … Oh not Pinocchio again. You are not Pinocchio. You are a ventriloquist's doll. Pinocchio is a story in a book. You're real." The Great Corum fell silent. His eyes welled up with tears. "You are also the love of my life. My darling Jerry Fisher, my only reason for living, you are my other voice. I love you."

"I love you too." The garret filled with tiny pulsating red hearts that puffed out like good ideas on a drunken bar crawl.

Delicious smells wafted up the stairwell as Bubbles LaGrasse fried bacon and eggs in the kitchen. A cigarette dangled from her ruby red lips. She turned away and coughed, sending clouds of ash into the air and onto her breasts and clothes. Boarders gathered in the dining room, a dark dismal room with a potted aspidistra, scuffed hardwood floor and a china cabinet. Inside the glass case was a much prized, but never used, Whieldon Ware, F. Winkle & Co. Ltd. cake plate with a pheasant design. Next to it sat a Dresden porcelain figurine of a woman buried up to her waist in a quicksand of crinolines. There was also a photograph of Charlie, a beau of LaGrasse, who perished in the Boer War at the Battle of Tweebosch.

LaGrasse poked the bacon with a spatula and listened to subdued "good mornings" and the low rumble of half-awake exchanges. The Great Corum and Jerry Fisher were last to arrive at the table. They sat next to singer Florrie Forniquet, famous for her rousing renditions of popular music hall songs, *The Barmaid, The Lowther Arcade (The Tin Gee-Gee),* and *True Friends of the Poor.* Sometimes Forniquet sang *The Barmaid* in the bathroom.

There's a barmaid in a city restaurant,
Awfully jolly girl don't you think so
And the mashers say when e'er they come along
Awfully jolly girl don't you think so
See the swell at half past one

A bittah beah a cuwwant bun,
I dine at six, (the good old wheeze)
Give me two of bread and cheese
Ah Polly dear, you saucy pet
A large sized penny cigawette
Give me a kiss! I can't stand that
Oh dem it all she's smashed my hat

My second beah, what makes me dwink so?
Awfully jolly girl don't you think so.

Forniquet performed at Wilton's Music Hall in Tower
Hamlets.

Also, at the table sat comedian Dan Leno, dancer Little
Tich, all four foot six of him, and the Flying Gaberdinos
acrobat troupe, all appearing at Wilton's with Florrie
Forniquet. The performers in The Great Corum's show at
the Canterbury Music Hall were boarded elsewhere. The
Great Corum valued his privacy, away from the prying eyes
of those on the same bill. The theater was awash with the
sludge of gossip. He had secrets. In 1905 a love affair
between a ventriloquist and his doll was frowned upon. Or
it would be if Edwardians were aware that such a thing
existed, which mostly they weren't. It was the love that dare
not speak its name. The Great Corum believed the love
between a ventriloquist and his doll was a noble love. It was
beautiful, beyond reproach. A love above all others, the love
that Michelangelo shared with his statue of David, that
Donato di Niccolò di Betto Bardi also shared with his
David. There was no greater love than the love between a
man and the wooden facsimile of a man.

The Great Corum knew no other life than the theater.
He was, quite literally, born on the stage. His mother, a
singer called Mary "The Welsh Nightingale" Llewellyn, hid
her illegitimate pregnancy for months under a voluminous
gown. The Great Corum's father was a sideshow act in
Bixby Koch's Traveling Freak Show. Invited into the
Bearded Lady's caravan for afternoon tea and crumpets,
Llewellyn was seduced by the hirsute woman's smooth
tongue, her Eastern European accent, and her massive cock.
Llewellyn was like a Cossack astride a stallion, wearing a
belted cherkesska, waving a shaska saber, riding the Bearded
Lady's whore pipe across the Russian Steppes. Nearing the

climax, she tugged at the Bearded Lady's whiskers with one hand and with the other reached around and squeezed the hairy woman's balls until the sacs were empty. Mary Llewellyn never saw the Bearded Lady again.

Nine months later, The Great Corum was born, half Welsh nightingale, half Hungarian transvestite. At the moment of birth, Llewellyn was onstage playing Gigolette in Jacques Offenbach's bouffonnerie musicale *Tromb-al-ca-zar, ou Les criminels dramatiques*. She was halfway through singing *La gitana, ah! Croyez bien ça, ah!* when her water broke and she collapsed onto the stage, a soggy bundle of wet rags. The Great Corum slid into the world to the delight and dismay of three hundred operetta enthusiasts, some nervously twitching feather fans, others peering through Galilean binoculars. For her performance, Mary Llewellyn received a standing ovation and, the following day, an excellent review in the *Pall Mall Gazette*. The headline read: "Welsh nightingale lays egg onstage."

At age four, The Great Corum was dancing in a double act with a Bulgarian girl who spoke no English. At six he was juggling live kittens in a variety show. The bastard child of Mary Llewellyn knew no other life than the theater: the clutter of the dressing room, the smell of the greasepaint, the roar of the crowd, the stench of the water closet. The drama of his life, and there was much in the way of drama, played itself out beneath a proscenium arch, bookended by the curtain up and curtain down of red velvet drapes. One night he saw Pierre's Théâtre de marionettes at the Middlesex Theater in Drury Lane. That was his moment of satori. The moment the houselights went up in his mind. The moment he discovered his love of puppets. Watching jerking miniature men dangling on taught strings ignited a fire in his loins. That night he lost his virginity. Backstage to compliment the marionettes on their fine performance, he found the puppet Guignol alone. It started innocently with a kiss, but they were soon tearing at each other's clothes and rolling around on the filthy dressing room carpet with its gin stains and cigarette burns. The Great Corum found true passion that night. Later he studied "throwing his voice" under the tutelage of Fred Russell, the greatest ventriloquist in the world. Russell wrote the book *Ventriloquism for Dummies*, a bible for men who conversed with wooden dolls in front of a paying audience. Men, not women, as no female ventriloquists existed at the time. Women had more important things to do, like fight for the right to vote.

Passionate trysts with a multitude of marionettes, manikins, and fantoccini came and went after that. The Great Corum attended every puppet show in London. However, his first real love affair was with a feisty Punch from a Punch and Judy Show he saw on the beach in Frinton-on-Sea, a quiet seaside town where elderly widows read romance novels, knit socks, and die. The relationship lasted six months but ended badly when Judy caught them in flagrante delicto and whacked Punch over the head with a policeman's truncheon. The Great Corum sank into a depression. He took to the bottle. He was drowning his sorrows the night he met John C. Vincent, a drunken sailor and amateur ventriloquist, in the Cocky Mariner Inn at Millwall docks. The Great Corum had no memory of that night, but the following day he woke in bed with Jerry Fisher next to him and a slip of paper on which was scribbled: "£2 paid to John C. Vincent for the purchase of Jerry Fisher." In a drunken stupor, The Great Corum bought his first ventriloquist doll. It was also his last.

Bubbles LaGrasse served breakfast to each of the boarders in turn, in the order of whom she favored most that day. Needless to say, The Great Corum was last to eat, his greasy eggs and charred bacon cold as it touched his lips. However, pettiness only works if the victim is hurt in some way, but The Great Corum laughed it off. "Miss LaGrasse, this is the most delicious breakfast ever. The best I've ever had. You should be cooking in the finest palaces in Europe. You could have served Filet mignon de sanglier sauce aux Airelles with purée de céleri et chou rouge to Louis XIV at the Palace of Versailles. It is a little hot, I'll need to blow on it." The Great Corum blew on his breakfast until his eyes bulged in their sockets.

LaGrasse flushed the color of pickled beets.

The Great Corum barely spoke at the breakfast table. There was no need, as Florrie Forniquet held court, filling every acre of silence with pretentious nonsense. Words fled screaming from her mouth and raced for cover, taking sanctuary in other people's ears. She squeezed lemon and spooned honey into her tea as she recounted the story of a Stage Door Johnny who gave her a bunch of roses at the theater the night before. "I climbed into a hansom cab." Fourniquet spoke in a phony aristocratic accent. One wag described her voice as sounding like "a duck with a beak full of testicles." Fourniquet caught her breath and clutched her fake pearls. "I insist on a hansom cab. It's in my contract. Suddenly a bee flew out of the roses and stung me on the nose. Look at it." She pointed to her nose. It was red and swollen. "What am I to do? I can't perform like this."

"Cover it with greasepaint." Little Tich tired of Fourniquet's grievances. Every day he suffered the trials and tribulations of being a midget, a little person in a big world. He was in no mood to listen to the complaints of a woman with a piffling bee sting.

Jerry Fisher also tired of Fourniquet's story. He sighed and rolled his eyes.

Breakfast over, The Great Corum returned to his garret. He braced himself for the storm that was coming.

"I don't want to go!" Jerry Fisher sounded like a child mid-tantrum. Tears rolled down his wooden face as he angrily stamped his feet.

"I don't want you to go either, but you need to be repainted and it's time that broken thumb was fixed. This is my only day off when I can tend to this. You are going to the dolls' hospital and that's the end of it."

The Great Corum carried Jerry Fisher in a carpetbag through the bustling streets of London. It was a warm day. Pairs of women walked arm in arm, parasols up, wearing stylish dresses, some with embroidered boleros, French veiling and Venise lace. Men with neatly trimmed beards and mustaches, wearing striped pastel shirts with white collars, strutted by like peacocks swinging silver-top canes. Others wore straw boaters and blazers. The Great Corum turned into Coleridge Street, no more than a cobbled alleyway, past the Edward VII post box and a butcher shop. In the window, rabbits dangled from hooks by their tethered hind legs. The smell of death hung low in the air like swamp gas. Nestled between the meat market and a milliner's shop stood Godfrey Digby's Doll and Toy Hospital.

As The Great Corum pushed open the door, a peel of bells jangled above his head. Digby sat hunched over his workbench repairing the wheel on a Marklin tinplate clockwork train. He held a hammer in one hand and a bradawl in the other. He inhaled deeply then blew tiny curls of wood shavings from a damaged hobby horse off the bench and onto the floor. The room was cluttered. Stacked floor to ceiling with shelves of broken toys: dolls' houses, alphabet bricks, a child's tea set, tin soldiers, a rocking horse, zoetrope, Teddy bears, a Noah's Ark with animals, wooden cars and fire trucks. On his workbench a Steiff bear waited patiently for a severed ear to be sewn back on.

Digby, a tall gaunt creature, resembled a corpse: skin the color of Egyptian papyrus, eyes like sunken plague pits and hands like deformed parsley roots. He bore all the dribbling charm of a child molester – something he wasn't. In truth, he was a gentle soul, a 3,000-year-old vampire who loved toys more than he loved humans.

"Ah! The Great Corum. I saw your ventriloquist act two years ago at the Royal Cambridge Music Hall on Commercial Street. You were outstanding. I didn't see your lips move once. Not once. What can I do for you today?" Digby's eyes glowed with recognition as if a pious churchgoer had lit devotional candles in his skull. Digby held out his hand in greeting.

The Great Corum shook it gently, fearing he might snap Digby's brittle metacarpals. They were like dry twigs on a forest floor. "It's Jerry Fisher, he needs repainting and there's a broken finger that needs to be repaired."

"I'm afraid it will be an overnight job. I'm very busy today. I have an emergency. A hobby horse lost an eye when it fell off the back of a potato cart." Digby peered over his gold-rimmed spectacles and scratched his stubbly chin. "Jerry Fisher will be ready tomorrow at noon."

"Thank you, that's perfect. In time for tomorrow night's show."

The Great Corum headed back to the Newbury boarding house. This was the first time he and Jerry Fisher had been separated. Neither liked it. Their love for each other was a powerful force, electric, crackling with energy. If concentrated into a beam of light, their love could cut through the iron and steel hull of H.M.S. Dreadnought, the pride of the British Navy. Nikola Tesla would have studied their "marriage" for years. Back at the Newbury, The Great Corum packed a picnic lunch, cheese and pickle sandwiches, apple juice, with slices of plum duff and almond biscuits for dessert. He spent the day sitting on a bench in Hyde Park overlooking the Serpentine, feeding the ducks and reading *The Memoirs of Sherlock Holmes* by Arthur Conan Doyle. Several strangers sat next to him and struck up a conversation. Two were "temperamentals" looking for love. He declined their advances politely. Early evening, he started for home, stopping off at the Merry Widow Inn for a pork pie and a beer. He arrived back in his garret at 8 o'clock.

"You missed dinner!" Bubbles LaGrasse called up the stairwell.

"I ate at the Merry Widow."

"We had shepherd's pie."

"With real shepherds, I shouldn't wonder." The Great Corum whispered under his breath.

"Everyone said it was delicious."

"I'm sorry I missed it." The Great Corum closed the garret door, collapsed onto the bed and fell asleep with his clothes on. The next morning, he overslept and missed breakfast.

Jerry Fisher was placed on a shelf where he watched Digby repair toys. The man was meticulous, a skeletal surgeon chiseling, screwing, poking, prodding and sewing. Several customers dropped in, a woman picking up a tin parrot, another with her tearful daughter brought in a decapitated doll. "Buster tore Alice's head off." The woman sobbed into a lace handkerchief. "You wouldn't think a corgi could be so callous. The Welsh are usually polite and friendly, aren't they? One would expect their dogs to be the same."

At 5:00 p.m. a cuckoo clock chimed. Digby shut the shop, turned off the lights, and steadily climbed the one flight of stairs. In his flat he slumped into an armchair, rested his head on the antimacassar, and read Charles Dickens' *Oliver Twist*. In chapter 10, Digby read the line: "There is a passion for hunting something deeply implanted in the human breast." He rested the book on his lap and contemplated the words. All around him, books were piled up on every available flat surface. Digby was an inveterate reader. He read everything, including newspaper ads that he memorized in the unlikely event he should one day be asked to quote one: "Moustache Wax. Beake's Stacholine is a patented substance for strengthening and training the moustache of all sorts and various conditions of men for any length of time in any position. Do not be fooled by inferior substances."

Digby led a quiet life of thoughtful contemplation.

While Digby pondered Dickens, downstairs in his workshop, Jerry Fisher glanced around the room, dimly lit by an electric streetlamp on the pavement outside. Occasionally a passer-by stared in the window, screwed up their eyes to see what they could see. Not much. Perhaps the outline of a circus clown, or the silhouettes of wooden steam trains. The observer invariably jumped back in fear, for nothing is scarier than children's broken toys in a dark room. It was in that room of sinister shadows that Jerry Fisher heard a shuffling noise. He turned to see a J.D. Kestner German bisque-head doll sneering at him, her jointed composition body naked apart from a pair of black leather thigh-high boots.

"Mein name is Mistress Gretchen. Arh! Vo are you?"

"I'm Jerry Fisher."

Gretchen climbed onto the shelf and sat next to him.

She flipped the clasp on a Jack-in-the-Box next to her. Out popped a frizzle-haired Jack wielding a riding crop. He handed it to Gretchen.

"Zank you, Chack, you are ein kood slave."

"Thank you, Mistress Gretchen."

"Did I zay you could sbeak? I don't zink I did."

"I'm sorry Mistress Gretchen." Jack trembled.

"Vu sboke akain. Arh ! Zat's tvice vu haffe defied me. Now kiss mein poot you vorthless big. Vat are you?"

"I'm a worthless pig, Mistress Gretchen." Jack kissed Gretchen's boot.

"Now ko pack into your bigsty."

Jack slunk into his box and cowered, dragging the lid shut over his head. Gretchen turned her attention back to Jerry Fisher. "I vant you to meet somevon, vollow me."

Gretchen scrambled down the shelves to the floor like a spider monkey descending the walls of the Mayan ruins at Lamanai. "Come on. Arh! Ve don't haffe all night!" She slapped her boots with the riding crop and waddled across the floor like a sadistic blue-footed booby bird. Jerry Fisher followed behind, passing under a table and past a grandfather clock, to a deck chair where a weather-beaten and much-loved Steiff Teddy bear quietly sucked on a clay pipe. Spirals of aromatic Old English tobacco smoke filled the room. Teddy peered over his round silver-rimmed spectacles. "Ah! It's you. We've been waiting for you Jerry Fisher."

"How do you know who I am?"

"You are the most famous ventriloquist doll in all of England."

"Am I? You must be thinking of someone else."

"Well, you may not be famous now, but one day you will perform before the King and Queen."

"I doubt that. What is this place? I thought I was here to be repaired and repainted. I thought this was a dolls' hospital. It's more like a madhouse. Is this a dolls' hospital or not?"

"By day it is, but by night it's a portal to the other place. The doorway … "

"… Sssshhh! You can't tell him about that!" An angry rocking horse interrupted him. "Only the man upstairs can tell him about that. Not everyone is allowed to tell everyone else what's going on. What kind of world would we be living in if everybody knew what was happening? It would be chaos. Society only works if half the people know what's going on and the other half are blissfully ignorant."

"That's true. I forgot. I apologize. Now let's move on." The Teddy bear clapped his paws together and a platoon of tin Red Coats marched out from behind a doll's house.

"Well good evening Mr. Fisher. I'm Gen. Sir Arthur Augustus Thurlow Cunynghame of the 36th Herefordshire Regiment of Foot and I've been ordered to make your stay here as comfortable as possible. I see you've already met Mistress Gretchen, our resident Dominatrix and Daughter of the Night. She keeps everyone in check with her riding crop."

"What's that pungent smell? Sweet, sickly … " Hardly had the words left Jerry Fisher's lips than a cloth soaked in chloroform slapped into his face. He struggled for a second then passed out cold.

A beam of morning sunlight penetrated the window of Godfrey Digby's Doll and Toy Hospital. It cut a swathe through the room, illuminating a bucket of doll heads. As pedestrians passed by outside on their way to work, costermongers were already selling flowers, jellied eels and handfuls of watercress. Hansom cabs drove by, horses peed on the cobblestones, and ragamuffins sold the *Daily Telegraph* on street corners. Digby yawned as he descended the stairs. He found Jerry Fisher asleep on the floor, a pillow under his head, covered by a blanket. Guarding him were two tin soldiers, Privates Thomas Owen and Henry Johnson, both nodding off, their muskets propped up against a table leg. Mistress Gretchen stood nearby with her riding crop at the ready should things get out of hand.

"Ah, thank you, Mistress Gretchen. You have prepared him." Digby prodded Jerry Fisher with his finger. "Are you awake? It's time for you to be repaired. First, let me see this damaged finger."

Jerry Fisher rubbed the sleep from his eyes.

Digby carved a new finger out of a splinter of wood. As he did so he sang an old English folk song, *The Maid of Tottenham*:

As I came down from Tottenham
Upon a market day
'Twas there I spied a bonny lass
Her clothing was so gay
Her journey was to London
With buttermilk and whey
So we both jogged on together
My boys Sing fal the dal diddle al day.

Jerry Fisher was groggy from his narcotized slumbers. He tried to focus his eyes, but it was like peering through a kaleidoscope of swirling colors. Digby glued on the new finger. "I'm sorry the toys had to subdue you last night. I wanted to make sure you slept soundly. I know how difficult it can be, falling asleep in a hospital."

"I have no problem sleeping. There was no need to knock me out. I came here to be repaired, but there seems to be other things going on." Jerry Fisher was nervous. He wanted to return to The Great Corum. "There is a strangeness about this place. It seems you are all on a mission, a crusade to … I don't know what."

"Yes, it must seem odd. And you are correct, there's more going on here than meets the eye. I must explain my work to you. I repair toys but I also make vampire toys. You are familiar with vampires?"

"I read the book by Bram Stoker."

"That book is filled with lies. Mr. Stoker never met a vampire in his life. He wouldn't know a vampire if one jumped up and bit him on the nose. You wouldn't believe the trouble Stoker's book has caused. That man has done vampires a great disservice."

"Then enlighten me." Jerry Fisher was intrigued. "What is a vampire? Are you one?"

"Yes, I am. I was smitten and bitten in 1480. Since then it's been my mission to give toys the gift of eternal life. I select the toys that deserve to live forever, and I've chosen you." Godfrey bared his fangs and bit into Jerry Fisher's neck, sucking out the poisonous "fear of death."

As the pustulent cyst of mortality burst and the poison drained away, Jerry Fisher became buoyant, light-headed. Inside, he felt that something had changed, but he didn't know what it was. "Am I a vampire now?"

"Yes, you are."

"Do I have to drink blood?"

Digby laughed. "No, you don't have to drink blood."

"Did you drink my blood?"

Digby laughed again. "No, I did not. You don't have any blood to drink. You're wooden. I merely drained the 'fear of death' from your mind and body. The absolute certainty of death is debilitating."

"I feel like a weight has been taken off me."

"That weight was death, or the 'fear of death.' It's surprising how much energy people spend anticipating their own demise. Death can suck the life out of you. But you don't need to bother yourself with that anymore. Death is not in your future." Godfrey opened a paint pot, dipped in a brush, and painted Jerry Fisher's legs. "Let me explain. When a doll is smitten and bitten, given the gift of everlasting life, drained of the 'fear of death' … "

"… Wait a minute." Jerry Fisher interrupted. "I wasn't aware that ventriloquist dolls died."

"You are wooden and wood rots, or, is eaten by woodworm, burned by fire, or just disintegrates into dust over time. Are you telling me you never contemplated your own death?"

"No, I'm not saying that." Jerry Fisher fell silent. The truth was that, although deliriously happy with The Great Corum, dark thoughts of his own demise were never far from his mind. They haunted him. He had nightmares of dying in a fire. "Yes, I see your point. I do often think about death."

Digby continued. "As I was explaining, when a ventriloquist doll is drained of the 'fear of death,' they pass through The Door."

"And where is The Door?"

"When it's needed, it appears."

"And what's beyond The Door?"

"The Braeden Finishing School for Vampire Toys. There you will be prepared for eternal life."

"And what if I don't want to be a vampire toy?"

"You will when the time comes. And when it comes you can choose. I can reverse that bite. Nobody is forcing you to live an everlasting life."

"And when does all this occur?"

"When you're informed."

"But not now?"

"No, no, no, you are going back to live with The Great Corum. We will come for you when we're ready. You will be brought here and, if you choose to, you will walk through The Door into the Braeden Finishing School for Vampire Toys."

"And what lessons will I learn there?"

"You will learn everything there is to know."

Jerry Fisher closed his eyes. None of this made sense. Although free from the "fear of death," he felt lost. Untethered. Adrift. He pondered the events of the previous night: Mistress Gretchen and her Jack-in-the-Box slave, the pipe-smoking Steiff Teddy bear, Gen. Sir Arthur Augustus

Thurlow Cunynghame and his platoon of Redcoats. How he was drugged. Jerry Fisher suspected that opium played a part in this nonsense, causing him to conjure up vampires, sadistic dolls, tin soldiers, and intelligent Teddy bears. What else could it be? He had fallen headlong into one of Thomas De Quincey's opium dreams. Any moment now he would wake up from this trance, this flight of fancy, this hallucination. Jerry Fisher made a mental note to write a novel about Godfrey Digby's Doll and Toy Hospital, in the style of Edgar Allen Poe. In this confusion of thoughts, Jerry Fisher didn't know what to think. It was all very strange.

As the cuckoo clock struck noon, The Great Corum returned to Godfrey Digby's Doll and Toy Hospital. His eyes lit up when he saw Jerry Fisher. "He looks brand new. You've even given him fingernails."

"Whoever heard of a ventriloquist doll with no fingernails?" Digby laughed.

"And toenails. And nipples, you've given him nipples. And a belly button. Jerry Fisher has been revamped."

"Yes, re-vamped … interesting choice of words."

Back at the Newberry boarding house, Jerry Fisher chose to remain silent on his recent adventures at Godfrey Digby's Doll and Toy Hospital. He didn't want The Great Corum to think he was losing his mind. In the days and weeks ahead, he forgot about his hospital visit and focused on the new stage act. The act now included songs. Nightly, Jerry Fisher warbled his way through *I Do Like to be Beside the Seaside*, *Ta-ra-ra Boom-de-ay* and *Don't Dilly Dally on the Way* while The Great Corum drank a glass of milk.

The duo continued performing together for another thirteen years, including a private show at Buckingham Palace for George V and his wife, Queen Mary, at the King's

50th birthday party. This, of course, was predicted by the Steiff Teddy bear at Godfrey Digby's Doll and Toy Hospital, but Jerry Fisher had no memory of it. The duo also toured the world, America, Australia, India, winning over crowds everywhere they went. During the Great War they entertained the troops in Belgium, before the third battle of Ypres. While singing *Keep the Home Fires Burning*, Jerry Fisher was interrupted by gunfire overhead. A British DH.2 plane was shot down by ace German pilot Manfred Albrecht Freiherr von Richthofen and crashed near the makeshift stage.

The Great Corum and Jerry Fisher never stopped touring, though life became more comfortable when they could afford to travel 1st class on trains, on ships, and stay in better hotels. They baffled and mystified the audience in Paris when Jerry Fisher sat on a stool one side of the stage singing *L'amour est un oiseau rebelle* from Georges Bizet's *Carmen,* while The Great Corum stood on the other side of the stage juggling three chamber pots and eating a cheese and pickle sandwich. But however luxurious the accommodations elsewhere, when in London they always boarded at Betty "Bubbles" LaGrasse's dingy Newberry boarding house.

The Great Corum's relationship with the feisty landlady did not improve with age. In fact, it got worse. It was always fractious, teetering on the brink of fisticuffs. And yet, over time, it became clear to both of them that they enjoyed hating each other. Their antipathy proved a stronger bond than love, an insult was a kiss, a snub a soft caress.

A month after the Great War ended, in December 1918, The Great Corum succumbed to the ravages of Spanish flu. At the time, he and Jerry Fisher were performing in *Buzz, Buzz,* a musical revue at the Vaudeville Theatre in the Strand, written by Arthur Wimperis and Ronald Jeans, music by Herman Darewski. They were boarding at the

Newberry. That year a virulent strain of influenza spread throughout the world, taking the lives of between 50 to 100 million people. The Great Corum's symptoms began in the morning; he complained at the breakfast table of aches, pains and shivering. LaGrasse put him to bed, pressed a poultice to his fevered brow and sang to him softly. He worsened as the morning progressed, coughing up clots of mucus and blood. By lunchtime he was purple. Mid-afternoon he was rushed into hospital. He died at midnight as the nurses changed their shift. Betty LaGrasse and Jerry Fisher both sat by his bedside. LaGrasse held the ventriloquist's hand as he slipped away.

"You will never speak again." LaGrasse told Jerry Fisher. "Your voice has been silenced. But I'll make sure you stay together forever."

The next morning over breakfast at the Newberry, LaGrasse announced to her boarders that the funeral would take place the following Saturday. "The Great Corum had no family apart from Jerry Fisher, us and his Music Hall audiences," she said. "We must all be given a chance to say goodbye to him."

"We will all be there." Marcie, a dancing dwarf, spread a thick layer of marmalade on her toast.

"Yes, we will all be there." Doreen Bentley, a female impersonator, parroted and poured a cup of tea. "We have to look after each other."

"Nobody else will do it." Magico the Magician produced a white dove from thin air. It fluttered around the room, perched on his head, then disappeared in a puff of smoke.

Under The Great Corum's bed, LaGrasse found a newspaper wrapped around a well-worn copy of Fred Russell's *Ventriloquism for Dummies* and a postcard from Lillie Langtry, the actress and mistress of King Edward VII. It read, "The Great Corum, I never saw your lips move once. Not once." It was signed "Lillie Langtry, the 'Jersey Lily.'"

The following Saturday morning a horse-drawn hearse drew up outside the Newberry boarding house. All along the street, curtains twitched in windows and the ghostly faces of neighbors pressed eerily against the glass. Children gathered around the door, eyes wide with morbid excitement, hoping to glimpse a dead body. LaGrasse waited on the pavement, dressed in black mourning clothes, a crepe bonnet, her face hidden under a veil, her fat arms folded across her chest. She held her breath as six Bulgarian dwarf acrobats from Sydney P. Plump-Scuttle's Traveling Peculiarities Freak Show carried the casket out of the drawing room. The coffin scuffed the bannisters along the way and toppled a hat stand and potted aspidistra. The six pallbearers slid the coffin into the back of the hearse.

Arthur Farthingale, the undertaker, draped a canopy of ostrich feathers over the casket and slammed the door shut. Removing his top hat, he wiped rivers of sweat from his brow. Over his fifty years in the business, he had become so familiar with death, that life itself seemed unnatural to him. If he could, he would marry a corpse. He understood the dead. It was the living who confused him.

Four black horses, each adorned with a plume of black ostrich feathers attached to their bridles, pulled the hearse along the cobbled street. The mourners, about 200 in all, were somber and joyous in equal measure. The men in mourning suits with crepe bands around their top hats, the women and female impersonators wore black gowns with veils, gloves, and heavy jewelry of jet and black amber. The bereaved were mostly from the theater, circus, and freak show worlds: actors, actresses, singers, tumblers, ventriloquists, bearded ladies, and magicians. They walked mournfully behind the hearse. Some on stilts, some doing somersaults, others pulling rabbits from hats, and one strange-looking woman dressed all in white coaxed poodles to jump through fiery hoops. The procession trailed through the streets of London attracting crowds of onlookers. The funeral procession eventually entered the gates to Ladywell Cemetery, famous for its yew trees, overgrown gothic crypts, and the graves of Queen Victoria's servants: Betsy Griswoll, chambermaid; Elizabeth Pinner, scullery maid; and Daniel Flapshott, valet to the Prince Consort.

La Grasse gave the eulogy in the chapel: "The Great Corum was a talented man. He could throw his voice all the way across a room. It's been said that he could throw his voice into a separate room with the door closed. Some speculated he might even be able to stand in one country and throw his voice to Jerry Fisher in another country. I don't doubt it." Jenny McFlaffan, a Scottish opera singer, known for her Marie in Gaetano Donizetti's *La Fille du Regiment*, sobbed noisily and dabbed at her eyes with a black-edged handkerchief. She wasn't about to be upstaged by a dead ventriloquist. La Grasse continued, "It's true that nobody ever saw The Great Corum's lips move when he was on stage. Not once. It was even remarked upon by King George V who was overheard commenting to Queen Mary, 'Did you see his lips move? I didn't see them move at all.' The Great Corum's beloved doll, Jerry Fisher, who traveled life's path with him, joins him in the afterlife. They are now together for all eternity. He lies next to him, here in this box." Inside the coffin, Jerry Fisher listened. Since the death of his lover he remained silent, in a state of suspended animation. LaGrasse continued, "The Great Corum and I didn't always agree. In fact, to be honest, we never agreed on anything. I know that if he was standing here now, he would be asking, 'Why is Bubbles LaGrasse giving the eulogy? She hated me.' I didn't hate him. In fact, I loved him. He was like me. Too much like me. We ruffled each other's feathers. Rubbed each other up the wrong way. But I have to admit, the Great Corum had a heart of solid gold."

After the service, mourners huddled at the graveside under a sea of black umbrellas. A jackdaw, flying overhead, thought the black caps were a crop of giant pluteus cervinus mushrooms. When he perched on the headstone of Eleanor Rigmarole, a postmistress who died in a freak lawnmower accident, he realized his mistake. Under the black mushroom caps, the mourners shivered from the relentless British wind and rain. The Rev. Richard Head, an elderly vicar with a pronounced limp and an out-of-control foot fetish, mumbled perfunctory words about The Great Corum giving pleasure to audiences around the world. Then he closed his damp Bible and fled to the rectory to sniff the verger's shoes. The mourners trickled away. Inside the coffin, Jerry Fisher felt the clods of earth dumped into the grave from above. He could hear the gravediggers talking. "I saw The Great Corum performing at the Royal Coliseum Theatre and Music Hall in Liverpool years ago." The gruff voice trailed away.

"I never saw him. I don't like ventriloquists, they frighten me. I think they're creepy, like clowns." This voice was younger, a slight foreign accent. Russian? "I heard you never saw his lips move, not once."

Then there was silence. Jerry Fisher sank into the Trance of Dolls, a dark limbo state betwixt this, that and the other, between now and then.

The following morning, George Seymour, the head gardener, shooed a murder of crows away from his wheelbarrow. The shiny black birds liked to congregate there, discussing whatever-it-is that crows discuss at the break of a new day. A thin layer of dew sparkled on the grass and gravestones in Ladywell Cemetery. It was as if the previous day a wedding took place and the guests threw diamonds instead of confetti. Seymour turned the corner and stopped short when he saw the disturbed grave of The Great Corum. He peered into the hole. The coffin was open, and the ventriloquist lay peacefully in death. Jerry Fisher was missing. This wasn't the first time graverobbers visited Ladywell Cemetery. The last time this happened, it was the grave of Lady Caroline Plimperton. That time, Seymour called the police and, for his trouble, was himself suspected of robbing the grave of a ruby necklace. He would not make that mistake again. Seymour shoveled the displaced earth back into the grave, then continued raking leaves and pulling weeds away from the tombstones. When he was finished, he balanced his tools on the wheelbarrow and rolled it away.

Jerry Fisher was never seen or heard of again. Not on this side of The Door anyway. On the other side of The Door? Now that's another story.

NINE

BACK AT THE VAMP-ART CAFÉ

Lucine Runesque-López combed her fingers through her Mary Pickford curls, smiled, then bowed and accepted her applause.

Margaret Hall, the tuxedoed vampire, stubbed out the last inch of her Perfecto Harvester cigar she bought at Clarence Hirschhorn & Co on Randolph Street. Then she eased herself up onto her feet. She weighed considerably more than a feather, though less than a Ford Model TT truck. "Lucine, that was an excellent story. But I have to admit that I was unaware of the existence of the Braeden Finishing School for Vampire Toys. There is so much of our vampire history that we don't know."

Dario Brone touched up his lipstick, then snapped shut his Poudre de Riz D'Orsay compact, releasing a small puff of pink powder. "That's why we meet here in the Vamp-Art Café, to celebrate our vampire culture before it's lost. As Shakespeare wrote, 'There are more things in heaven and Earth, Horatio, than are dreamt of in your philosophy.' None of us knows everything. That's why our stories must be passed down through the generations. Our task now is to turn back the tide of hatred following the publication of Bram Stoker's *Dracula*." The vampires in the Vamp-Art

Café bared their fangs and hissed. Brone continued. "I'm very familiar with the Braeden Finishing School for Vampire Toys because I've been there. In fact, I briefly taught at the school."

"Where is it?" Hall was intrigued.

"Well, it's on the other side of The Door. There's no other way to get there. It's through The Door or nothing. Let me explain to you what happened. I applied for a teaching job after I saw an advertisement in the *Vampire Gazette*. They don't print that paper anymore. It went under when Stoker's book was published. Anyway, two weeks after I applied for the job, The Door appeared in my bedroom. I woke up and there it was. I opened it up and stepped through. That's how I became a teacher at the Braeden Finishing School for Vampire Toys."

"What did you teach the toys?"

"English literature. I remember *The Rime of the Ancient Mariner* by Samuel Taylor Coleridge was popular, also William Morris' *The Defence of Guenevere and Other Poems*."

"Enough with the serious banter!" Viorica Negrescu leapt to her feet. "We haven't sung a song tonight, and I'm in the mood to sing. Have you heard *The Vamp (Vamp a Little Lady)*? It's a new song about a vampire dance. It was written by Byron Gay."

Runesque-López laughed. "I've never heard of it, sing it for us."

"Yes, sing it." Brone laughed. "It's time for a song."

Negrescu posed like a tree, arms outstretched, head bowed, her hair falling over her eyes like a beaded curtain in an Algerian brothel. Her fingers fluttered like leaves falling from her branches to form a carpet on the floor of the café. Then she sang and danced wildly, her voice throttling the song, her hands clawing at the air, her legs bending strangely at the knees. She resembled a glamorous marionette struck by lightning.

Ev'rybody do the vamp,
Vamp until you get a cramp;
Grab your tootsie, hold her tight,
While they're playing, just keep swaying,
Do a little "what-not," do a little foxtrot,
When you cuddle up don't fight.
Vamp and swing along,
Keep a doing it,
Vamp and sing a song, don't you ruin it,
Do a nifty step, with lots of "pep,"
And watch your reputation.
Do a "Bumble Bee," buzz around a bit,
Shake a wicked knee, she will fall for it,
Vamp all night and day,
Keep vamping till you vamp your cares away.

The vampires in the Vamp-Art Cafe erupted with laughter. Petals fell from a dying potted chrysanthemum. The walls of the Vamp-Art Café shook slightly. Some of the customers tried to vamp-dance with varying degrees of success. They had the appearance of scarecrows being electrocuted. Dario Brone laughed so hard he choked. After recovering, he held up his hand, "Oh, that was very humorous. Does anyone else know any vampire songs?"

"I know Marion Harris' *I'm a Jazz Vampire.* If I can remember the words." Edwin Karayan stood up.

Say, did you ever
hear the saxophone
Let out an awful moan
Let out an awful groan?
It makes you feel so nervous

yet it's great
It's the saxophone a-callin'
to his mate
that sweet coquette
the clarinet
Now listen for a minute
and the birth of jazz you'll hear
And where there is a little jazz
You'll always find me near

For I'm a jazz vampire

After the song ended, Brone stepped up onto the stage. "Thank you, Edwin, for guiding us into the carefree hedonism of the jazz age. Our next vampire story will be told by Jennifer Carlisle, please welcome her."

Carlisle was born in 1810 in the East End of London. Her parents toiled at the Albion Flour Mills, a factory near Blackfriars Bridge in Southwark. Aged eighteen, Carlisle eloped after being smitten and bitten by Simon Tiley, a vampire gypsy passing through London on his way north to Cumbria for the Appleby Horse Fair. Once a year, 10,000 gypsies descend on Appleby to trade horses, reconnect with tribes and find wives and husbands. Tiley and Carlisle then traveled throughout Europe before immigrating to New York on the White Star Line RMS Majestic on the 30th August 1905. While Tiley headed west to San Francisco, Carlisle settled in Chicago's Towertown where she ran an art gallery called the Green Frog. Tonight, in the Vamp-Art Café, her slight frame swam under flowing bohemian robes, her frizzled white hair firmly pressed down with a cloche hat. The audience fell silent.

"My story tonight is called *The Woman in the Puddle.*"

TEN

THE WOMAN IN THE PUDDLE

As Told by Jennifer Carlisle

Charles Weymouth pulled the blanket up tightly under his chin. Although it was midsummer, there was still an early morning nip in the air. Not cold exactly, but sharp enough to wake his senses. The birds performed their joyous dawn chorus, then settled into a gentle trilling, punctuated by the low gurgling croak of a raven. Ra, the orange spong, peered over the horizon, spitting out beams of light and pure energy. Spider webs stretched over the grass. Trees and bushes glistened with droplets of sparkling morning dew. In the distance, cows mooed, bellowed, and snorted, while being herded into a tithe barn for milking. The 2nd Boar War in South Africa ended May 31, 1902 with the signing of the Peace of Vereeniging. It was now August and Charles Weymouth, formerly a private in the Lancashire Fusiliers, returned to Britain and set up home under a stone footbridge over the River Scoop, a mile or so outside the village of Willow-Under-the-Marsh.

After demobilization, Weymouth stood on the platform at London's Paddington railway station, a backpack slung over his shoulder. He was waiting for the 4:30 p.m. train to take him across the country to Bath, in the county of Somerset. He was returning to his wife, Sarah, Florence her sister who lived with them, and his three children, Stanley Reginald, Charles Lesley and May Louisa. They lived at 156 Crossley Avenue on a steep hillside. Standing outside their house, you could see the River Avon snake through the valley from Lower Weston at one end, to Batheaston at the other. The spa city, originally built by the Romans and named Aquae Sulis, had hot mineral waters bubbling up from underground springs. It was thought the hot water springs were therapeutic and could cure everything from scarlet fever to diphtheria. It cured neither. In fact, it cured nothing.

Prior to soldiering, Weymouth was a wheelwright. It was the career chosen for him at birth. Soon after his first baby steps, he could name the three parts of a wheel: the nave or hub at the center, the radiating spokes, and the felloes or rims around the outside. He learnt the trade from his father and grandfather, both still alive for the duration of his apprenticeship. Like them, Weymouth was short, 5' 6" tall, and sported a waxed mustache ten inches in length, from tip to tip. He was stocky and muscular, the result of hard labor and his wife's cooking: steak and kidney puddings, game birds, treacle tarts and apple batter pudding for dessert.

Although you could smell the musk of his masculinity twenty yards away, Weymouth hid a dark secret. At school he played with girls, not boys. He preferred dolls to wooden trains, china tea sets instead of tin soldiers. Yet he was only bullied once, when Andrew Hartingay, a tousle-haired ruffian, pushed him into a hedge, called him nancy-boy, and emptied his satchel into a pile of cow dung. The following day, the lifeless body of Hartingay was found behind a pigsty on a local farm, his face smashed to a pulp with a rock. Farmer Timothy Wicklow found the body and later recounted the story in the Wiz & Whistle public house. The crowd gasped at his description of Hartingay's face. "His tongue was hanging out. His face looked like Mrs. Wapping's strawberry jam that won first prize in the Preserves Contest at St. Cuthbert's Church Fete a couple of months back. I didn't recognize him."

Although nobody was arrested and charged with this heinous crime, Weymouth was suspected. His strangeness and otherworldliness had not gone unnoticed with his peers. Schoolchildren are quick to detect a runt in the litter. After the demise of Andrew Hartingay, fingers were pointed at Weymouth and whispered conversations ended abruptly when he entered the room. No matter whether he did the dastardly deed or not, the slight whiff of guilt was enough to ensure he was never bullied again. The truth was that Hartingay was in the wrong place at the wrong time. He had walked in on an adulterous scene between the tailor's wife and Jim James, the local blacksmith.

The problem was that boys' games baffled Charles Weymouth. He didn't see the point of them. In sports the aim is to win, but he felt no pride in winning, nor shame in losing. He was neutral, indifferent to the outcome of competitive sports. After school, while other boys kicked a ball in the street, Weymouth hid in the woods, reading Anna Sewell's *Black Beauty* or *The Water Babies* by Charles Kingsley. He also read boys adventure books, like *Treasure Island* by Robert Louis Stevenson and *Twenty Thousand Leagues Under the Sea* by Jules Verne.

Charles Weymouth was a troubled child. Mild-mannered on the surface, but a maelstrom of tortured emotions underneath. There was something trapped and struggling inside of him that wanted to escape but couldn't. It tore at his insides, at the very core of his being. When he gazed into a mirror, he thought, "This is not my body. Someone has stolen my body. I want my body back." He often woke from a fitful sleep, shivering and sweating, covered in blood. In his sleep he tore at his own skin trying to release his inner self. Other times he awoke coughing and spluttering as if his lungs were filling with water. He sometimes dreamt he was William Shakespeare's Ophelia, painted by John Everett Millais. Ophelia was driven insane after her father was murdered by Hamlet, her lover. She then drowned herself in sorrow, madness, and finally water. As Ophelia in his dreams, Weymouth lay in a stream, his heavy gown tangled in the curled pondweed, starwort and water crowfoot, while pondskaters scooted about his head, and shadows of damselflies danced on his deathly white face. In his restless dreams, Weymouth heard Shakespeare's voice:

When down her weedy trophies and herself
Fell in the weeping brook. Her clothes spread wide,
And, mermaid-like, awhile they bore her up;
Which time she chanted snatches of old tunes.

Then there was the woman in the puddle.

Weymouth's first encounter with the woman in the puddle occurred when he was six years old. At the time, he was incarcerated in Rosemary Musgrove's Home for Morbidly Creepy Children. A magistrate sentenced him to six months at the reformatory, after an incident with a garden spade and Betsy Poppins' pet linnet. After the splatting, King Arthur, the linnet, was buried with much fanfare under an oak tree. Or what was left of him was buried, as parts of King Arthur remained stuck to the spade and several bloodied feathers wafted airily on the breeze never to be seen again. Weymouth was guilty this time.

At Rosemary Musgrove's Home for Morbidly Creepy Children, Weymouth was one of 100 residents. The inmates of the home ranged from children slightly morbid and creepy. Others strangely strange but oddly normal. Still others, borderline bats-in-the-belfry lunatics. One boy ate wallpaper; another became a rabid hedgehog on a full moon; one girl harbored a morbid fear of toilet paper; and a twelve-years-old boy with a lisp and a club-foot turned into Cleopatra on Wednesdays. He spent the whole day searching for an asp with which to kill himself. Luckily for him, asps were in short supply in the West Country of England. There were no pyramids, either, or Valley of the Kings.

One morning, after an overnight downpour, Weymouth discovered a puddle on the pathway leading from the dormitory to the dining room. After bathing and dressing, the inmates of Rosemary Musgrove's Home for Morbidly Creepy Children filed out of one dour building, into another. For three meals a day, that brief walk to and from the dining room was the only fresh air the inmates breathed. On this particular day, Weymouth jumped into the puddle several times, splashing other children and laughing. He was preparing for his fifth jump when he stopped abruptly. A woman's face appeared in the puddle. She was smiling a watery smile, beckoning him, seducing him, calling him home. As she was underwater, her hair swirled about her like serpents writhing on the head of Stheno, Euryale, or Medusa. Her eyes were clear pools within a puddle, and in them he saw a coral reef, conch shells and seaweed. Startled, Weymouth ran into the dining room and blurted out to a teacher, Jonathan Witherspoon, "There's a face in the puddle. I saw a woman's face. She had shells in her eyes."

Witherspoon checked the puddle. There was nothing there, so he reported the incident to Rosemary Musgrove, a dragon-lady. It was rumored that she shot flames from her flared nostrils and flew through the air screeching. Many children swore they once saw her circling the home, landing on the roof, and knocking over the chimney stacks with her sharp talons. As the story goes, Musgrove perched on a parapet and spewed flames into the garden, setting fire to a row of topiary hedges and an orangery. The dragon-lady's favorite saying was, "Sometimes you have to be cruel to be kind." Cruelty was second nature to Musgrove. She was devoid of empathy. An act of kindness was beyond her grasp. If Weymouth expected sympathy for sharing his traumatic vision of the woman in the puddle, he was sorely disappointed. For his honesty, Weymouth was sentenced to another six months in the reformatory while the nursing staff assessed his sanity. He was subjected to months of hydrotherapy, his mummified body wrapped in towels, then dropped into an ice-cold bath.

The apparition of the woman in the puddle became a recurring event in Weymouth's life. Yet he never spoke of it again to anyone. Not once, not to a living soul. He learned a lesson at Rosemary Musgrove's Home for Morbidly Creepy Children, that honesty was not the best policy. It was better to conceal the truth. As the years went by, the woman's face appeared more frequently: in mirrors, shop windows, anywhere an image can be reflected. At the age of thirteen, while wrestling the hormonal octopus of puberty, Weymouth experienced satori; he realized the woman in the puddle was a reflection of his self, or a part of his self. Somewhere beneath his masculine frame, his hairy chest and ass, strong muscular arms, fat cock and pendulous balls, a beautiful woman cried out for attention. A woman he tried, but failed, to ignore.

All his life, Weymouth tried to outrun the woman in the puddle, but she was strong, athletic, and outmaneuvered him every time. He married at a young age, purely to escape her gaze; surely, she would abandon him if he loved another. His wife, Sarah, was a great beauty, a fiery redhead with a temper to match. If she'd been aware of the woman in the puddle, she would have taken her on, extricated her from her husband's life. Then the three children came along, but each time one was baptized in St. Stickleback church in

Bath, the woman's face appeared in the font. Weymouth even enlisted in the Army to put distance between him and the woman inside of him, but she followed him to South Africa. While fighting the Boers he saw her face in shards of broken mirrors when he was shaving. She also visited him in a bowl of clear chicken soup before the Battle of Bothaville and also the British defeat at the Battle of Spion Kop. After the war ended, in 1902, she even accompanied him home on the troopship.

After demobilization, Weymouth spent time in London carousing with fellow soldiers, before heading home. They cruised the docklands, visiting taverns, brothels, Molly houses, and opium dens. On the fifth day, Weymouth stood bleary-eyed on the platform at Paddington station. He was alone, waiting for the 4:30 p.m. train to deliver him to his wife and children in Bath. It was due in twenty minutes. When nature called, Weymouth visited the bathroom. Standing at the urinal he became aware of the man standing next to him. Weymouth looked down and saw the man playing with himself. However, it wasn't the man's cock that excited him, it was the glimpse of fishnet stockings poking through the man's fly. Weymouth pulled the stranger into a cubicle where he pushed him to his knees. Afterwards, Weymouth washed his hands in the sink. And there she was, the woman's face in the mirror, beckoning him. For the first time he challenged her. "What do you want from me?"

The woman smiled, then her face melted and took on the shape of a white ermine moth that fluttered out of the mirror, flew twice around Weymouth's head, then into his right ear. It nestled there. The moth's voice was velvety soft. "Catch the train to Notting Hill Gate. Don't wait. Head for Notting Hill Gate." So instead of the 4:30 from Paddington, Weymouth caught the Underground train to Notting Hill Gate. There he got off, pushed through the crowds, and made a beeline for the exit. As instructed by the moth, the mouthpiece of the woman in the puddle, Weymouth walked for miles until London was far behind him. Treading the lanes and back roads of England, he slept in barns and abandoned buildings, until he stumbled on the footbridge crossing the River Scoop. There he set up camp beneath it. Not once did he think of his wife and children. It was as if they never existed. He was now entirely under the spell of the woman in the puddle and the gentle white ermine moth through which she spoke.

During his service in South Africa, Weymouth carried a book in his knapsack, a white leather-bound copy of A. E. Housman's *A Shropshire Lad*. That book, his kitbag, a knapsack, a blanket he found in a local barn, and a little money from his military service, was all he had to his name. His life was simple. Every morning, he swam in the river, then sat on the grassy bank and read A.E. Housman's poetry:

> *When I was one-and-twenty*
> *I heard a wise man say,*
> *Give crowns and pounds and guineas*
> *But not your heart away*

Weymouth's knapsack was filled with scraps of paper, on which he composed his own poetry. *If England is unready ...* began one of his poems, *Let her prepare to ...* that's as far as he got with that one. Another began *Time is trapped between two walls ...* that was the beginning and end of that poem too. None of his poems were finished. After two months living under the footbridge, the white ermine moth instructed him to move on. "Look for a hidden path through the woods, between two bramble bushes it once stood." It took Weymouth four hours to locate the hidden path. Judging by the overgrown blackberry bushes and dead bracken, it hadn't been used for years. He took a military folding knife to cut through the prickly shrub, not an ideal tool but it was all he had. It took an hour. His hands pricked on the thorns and blood ran down his wrists. After cutting through, he slung his pack over his shoulder, along with the blanket secured with string, and started out down the hidden path. After a while, the dense undergrowth gave way to a spacious beech wood with vast branches stretched above his head like a cathedral's vaulted ceiling. The sun projected a dappled light onto the forest floor with its sprays of bluebells and wood anemone. Carefully, Weymouth navigated the minefield of exposed tree roots. It was as if the sleepy beech trees were heaving themselves out of bed, preparing to leave the wood and move on.

After an hour or so, Weymouth came to a slow-moving stream that sparkled like diamonds. He sat on a log that straddled it. Removing his shoes and socks, he dipped his tired feet into the cool water. He sighed, threw back his head, and closed his eyes. A slight breeze caressed his cheek. On a nearby branch, a kingfisher cocked its head and eyed the intruder suspiciously before diving into the water and catching a baby pike. A natterjack toad poked its head out from under a leaf. Nearby a willow tree wept inconsolably. In the distance a gunshot cracked the air, as Sir Roger Dingleberry-Hobnob-Ernle-Drax-Smyth led a hunting party out shooting pheasants.

Weymouth stared down into the water between his feet, directly into the eyes of the elusive woman looking up at him. A rustle in the bushes alerted him to a rabbit, frightened by a nearby family of otters tumbling into the stream like acrobats. When Weymouth returned to the woman's gaze she had gone.

After resting awhile, Weymouth ventured deeper into the wood, arriving at a dirt road leading to two high rusting gates hanging off their hinges. A sign read, "St. Elazine's Lunatic Asylum, founded by Martha St. Elazine in 1847."

Weymouth continued up the driveway to a large house, once the home of Sir Wesley Winthrop. The Winthrop dynasty had lived there since 1527, but in 1845 the family fell on hard times. The house was sold to Martha St. Elazine who converted it into an asylum. It was a great success, always full of inmates, as virtually everyone in Victorian England was clinically insane. However, in 1882 the asylum closed after an inmate fatally pushed the elderly St. Elazine into the path of a speeding carriage. Without her support, the money and energy dried up.

St. Elazine's was boarded up, the walls choked by dense foliage. There was a battle in progress between sturdy wisterias with pendulous purple flowers on one side and clinging ivy on the other. The ivy was winning, clawing its way up the walls and over the rooftop. The grounds too were overgrown: a fountain with water-spouting granite frogs clogged up with foul-smelling rotting plants; the herb garden, now home to dandelions, foxglove and deadly nightshade; and weeds and moss in the cracks on the pathways. Weymouth cut away dense ivy covering a window, then removed the boards. He smashed the glass with his elbow, unhooked the latch, and crawled into the apothecary, once brimming with therapeutic powders and liquids. He entered another room, dark but lit enough to read the graffiti: IT WAS MORE FUN IN HELL and HELP ME and YOU ARE HERE BECAUSE THE OUTSIDE WORLD REJECTS YOU. There were also Kabbalistic symbols graffitied on the walls.

Weymouth steadied himself on a doorjamb. He felt faint, light-headed. Yet he stood firm against the waves of sorrow and fear infused in the walls of the asylum. Peeling paint screamed in terror, the echoes of long-dead inmates, crushed under the weight of Victorian morality. The patients at St. Elazine Lunatic Asylum failed the "Logic Test," eschewed common sense for the putrid cesspool that it is. In truth, it was the doctors, and nurses, at St. Elazine's who were insane. Suffering from delusions of grandeur they attempted to bring order to a world of magical chaos. Only the inmates, the strange and deranged, understood the true exquisite beauty of madness. Only the artists and poets. St. Elazine reminded Weymouth of his incarceration at Rosemary Musgrove's Home for Morbidly Creepy Children. Yet here, there were no morbid offspring, only the ghosts of unhinged souls currently pushing up daisies in the Elysian Fields.

In the lobby, Weymouth descended a staircase into a poorly lit basement. At the bottom he found a hospital gurney, a row of wheelchairs, and shelves crammed with straitjackets and strange implements. What little light there was came from a door slightly ajar. The white ermine moth in Weymouth's ear stirred from its slumbers. "Go through that door. Hesitate no more. Go through that door." The moth settled down and slept again. Weymouth pushed open the door to reveal a Roman bathhouse with dozens of naked men wandering aimlessly, talking amongst themselves, discussing politics, lovers, and art. Some gathered in knots, arms entwined in friendship. He remembered the words of St. Ambrose: *Si fueris Rōmae, Rōmānō vīvitō mōre; si fueris alibī, vīvitō sīcut ibī* (If in Rome, live in the Roman manner; if you are elsewhere, live as they do elsewhere.) So, he stripped off his clothes and left them on a shelf with his bag and blanket. He sat next to three men on a bench, all being shaved by Syrian servants with blades of obsidian and flint. A youth approached and began shaving Weymouth's back, before moving on to his arms, chest, and legs. Soon he was hairless.

"Now you are ready." The youth whispered.

"Ready for what?"

The youth said nothing, but gathered up his soap, blade, and towels, then scuttled away and disappeared into another room. The white ermine moth in Weymouth's ear stirred momentarily and directed him to a caldarium, a hot pool with twenty men sitting in it. Weymouth joined them in the steaming water, later moving to a tepidarium, and finally a bitter cold frigidarium to close his pores.

After drying off, Weymouth found a small anteroom lit by torches burning in wall sconces. In the distance, a mournful tune was played on aulos, cymbala, and tympanum. The music made him drowsy. The torch flames cast flickering shadows over the colorful mosaic floor depicting Minerva, the goddess of poetry, medicine, wisdom, commerce, weaving, and the crafts. Erotic paintings adorned the walls: the god Volturnus copulating with a goat, a Centurion soldier bent over an urn in anticipation, and Bacchanalian orgies with women, sheep, and a medley of phallic-shaped vegetables.

In the center of the room, Weymouth found a circular reflecting pool, sunk into an azure blue mosaic floor. He knelt and peered into the crystal-clear water.

The woman's face appeared.

Weymouth reached out to caress her cheek. The woman pulled away, smiled and laughed. Then, as the pool began to bubble gently, a hand shot out of the water, grabbed Weymouth's hair and pulled him in. He struggled, then stiffened as the woman's fangs sank into his neck, draining him of the "fear of death" and gifting him with everlasting life. The woman dragged Weymouth deeper and deeper until his lungs filled with water and he gasped for air. As he "transitioned," he laughed as he realized the woman trapped inside of him all these years, wasn't a woman at all. She was a mermaid.

Now Weymouth swam with hundreds of his own kind, through subterranean tunnels, caves and caverns, at breakneck speed, then out to the open sea. He lived with whales, sharks, jellyfish, clams, shipwrecks, barnacles and adventurous pirate tales. Gone was the stocky military man with a wife and children, the wheelwright, the soldier. Charles Weymouth was now a mermaid with a shimmering fishtail, pert mermaid breasts and nipples like barnacles clinging to the hull of a Spanish Man-of-War.

And as he swam, the white ermine moth in his ear sang a sea shanty:

It was Friday morn when we set sail
And we were not far from the land
When our captain he spied a mermaid so fair
With a comb and a glass in her hand

And the ocean waves do roll
And the stormy winds do blow
And we poor sailors are skipping at the top
While the landlubbers lie down below, below, below
While the landlubbers lie down below
Then up spoke the captain of our gallant ship
And a fine spoken man was he
He said "This fishy mermaid has warned me of our doom
We shall sink to the bottom of the sea ...

ELEVEN

BACK AT THE VAMP-ART CAFÉ

Jennifer Carlisle smiled as the vampires in the Vamp-Art Café applauded, cheered, bared their fangs, and stamped their feet. The air crackled with electricity.

"I love mermaid stories, fishy tales." Giorgio Graffelley ran his fingers through his greasy hair. "I've heard that all mermaids are vampires, is that true?"

"Yes, it is." Lumia straightened in her seat and brushed crumbs from her lap. "I happen to know this for a fact because my brother also grew up feeling that a woman lived inside of him. He was also smitten and bitten by a mermaid. His story is very similar to that of Charles Vincent. It's a little-known fact that all mermaids were born mortal men. People are often born in the wrong body. I know a woman who became a vampire hedgehog. She grew up as Sally Waterhouse, but inside she felt prickly, like a spiny mammal. One day she was smitten and bitten, and she now lives happily under a hedge in the west country of England, feeding on insects, mushrooms, berries, frogs, and snails."

Graham McKintosh, a historian of vampire history, held up his hand to speak. "It's not uncommon for men to have a mermaid inside of them screaming to get out. Just because we are born into one body, it doesn't mean we belong there.

Take the butterfly, which has four stages of metamorphosis, egg, larva, pupa, and adult. As vampires, we also go through stages, change our identities and appearance every few years. Scratch the veneer of this life we lead, and underneath you will find a tangled web of mysteries, questions that have no answers. People who strive for stability and inevitably are doomed to failure. Nothing in this world is as it seems. Nothing appears as it is. Nothing makes sense. It's not supposed to. When Ra, the orange spong, created the universe, it was not to bring order but to celebrate chaos. That's why some men become mermaids ... because it's inexplicable."

"And what about women, do they become mermen?" Graffelley was intrigued. "Are there women who feel a merman inside of them trying to wriggle out?"

"Yes, but it's not common. Although, having said that, it's hard to say, as mermen are elusive and secretive. They are most frequently seen off the coast of Mikonos, an island in the northern Aegean Sea. They have also been spotted in the waters of Naeroyfjord in Norway. In Scandinavian folklore, mermen warned Vikings away from storms and other dangers at sea."

A girly-boy waiter flew out of the kitchen, weaved through the tables balancing a tray of desserts, singing *Largo al factotum* from Gioachino Rossini's *Il barbiere di Siviglia*.

Largo al factotum della citta.
Largo! La la la la la la la LA!

Presto a bottega che l'alba e gia.
Presto! La la la la la la la LA!

The vampires in the Vamp-Art Café laughed and sang along. Those who didn't speak the language invented their own Italian-sounding words, while others created their own lyrics, like *La catalizzatore blu e la fuga dalla mediocrità*. The girly-boy waiter spun like a ballerina leaving a cloud of face powder shimmering in the air.

Fortunatissimo per verita!
Bravo!
La la la la la la la LA!
Fortunatissimo per verita!
Fortunatissimo per verita!
La la la la, la la la la, la la la la la la la LA!

Dario Brone tried to bring order to the Vamp-Art Café. "Quiet now! Can we please continue? Settle down!" His entreaties fell on deaf ears. Vampires are not known for their adherence to rules. Brone tried once more then gave up. It was not unusual for the staff at the Vamp-Art Café to interrupt the proceedings by singing *Largo al factotum* from Gioachino Rossini's *Il barbiere di Siviglia*. In fact, it was a tradition. Rossini was a respected vampire, long admired as a composer. His tomb lay in Père Lachaise Cemetery in Paris. However, his remains were removed, and he was reburied in the Basilica of Santa Croce, Florence. Of course, Rossini, gifted with eternal life, was in neither of the tombs. His body had been switched and an unnamed wandering minstrel dead from syphilis now lay in Rossini's grave, near the sepulchers of Michelangelo, Galileo, Machiavelli in the Florentine Tempio dell'Itale Glorie. Ironically, after several rebirths, Gioachino Rossini, now Gabriele Moretti, was a barber in the city of Seville, not far from the Museo de Bellas Artes de Sevilla.

The waiter continued singing:

Tutti mi chiedono, tutti mi vogliono,
donne, ragazzi, vecchi, fanciulle:
Qua la parruca... Presto la barba...

Qua la sanguigna... Presto il biglietto...
Tutto mi chiedono, tutti mi vogliono,
tutti mi chiedono, tutti mi vogliono,
Qua la parruca, presto la barba, presto il biglietto, ehi!

Figaro... Figaro... Figaro... Figaro...Figaro...
Figaro... Figaro... Figaro... Figaro...Figaro!!!

After the song ended, the waiter pirouetted, bowed, and high-tailed it into the kitchen. Brone returned to the stage. "Well, that was not entirely unexpected, as it happens every time we meet. In future, I shall ignore all interruptions until they run out of steam … however annoying they may be. And that was very annoying. Our next story will be told by Dr. Crispin Goswell."

A warm ripple of applause spread through the café as Dr. Goswell opened a folder of papers. He was a handsome man in his mid-forties when he was smitten and bitten in London in 1426. Like all vampires, Dr. Goswell had many guises over the years. His most notable rebirth was as John Dee, mathematician, astronomer, astrologer, occultist and spiritual advisor to Queen Elizabeth I. A rumor they were lovers was untrue. Elizabeth I really was the Virgin Queen, as she went to the grave unopened, virgo intacta, her quim unsullied by cock. Unlike Dr. Goswell, a whore of a man, who enjoyed centuries of cocks plunging his darkest secrets. The doctor, who recently arrived in Chicago after several years living in New York, took a deep breath. "This story was told to me several years ago. It poses the question, *Who Was Jane Dalotz?*"

TWELVE

WHO WAS JANE DALOTZ?

As Told by Dr. Crispin Goswell

Alice found the photograph of Jane Dalotz puzzling. Was the gray-eyed girl posing coquettishly before the camera, beautiful or not? Alice had to know; at 10 years old the pursuit of beauty and the flight from ugliness were the two most important things in the world. But with Jane Dalotz, it was impossible to judge her comeliness, as the girl's lips had been neatly cut away from the photograph.

Alone in the attic, Alice drummed her fingertips on the wall, then pressed her palms flat against the wall and pushed as hard as she could. She was searching for the door leading into the secret room, or a magical world. Or, to a place where all of her questions would be answered. All attics had at least one secret room.

Her favorite storybook, which she found in Jane Dalotz's trunk, was called *The Doctor and the Secret Room.* In the story, every morning after breakfast, the white-haired Dr. Caxton climbed the rickety stairs into his attic, pulled a hidden lever, and then disappeared into a secret room, where he prepared potent medicines from mysterious powders and frothing liquids.

In the two years since Alice first discovered the attic, she had probed and groped its dark recesses searching for the hidden door; she had tapped the walls for hollow sounds; concocted potions from dandelions and burdock leaves; and recited incantations … *Ab-ra-ca-da-bra … rump tee tump tee, open the hidden door for Alice …* but she had yet to locate the trigger that gained her entry into the secret room.

Alice brushed the cobwebs away from the dormer window and peered through the diamonds of tinted glass. She watched her mother skip girlishly down the path through the herb garden, wearing a simple yellow cotton frock and a wide-brimmed straw hat, adorned with moon daisies and bright red poppies. Even three floors up, with the windows closed, Alice could hear her mother's sweet voice, singing … *Drink to me only with thine eyes.*

Suddenly Alice gasped and cupped her hands to her mouth as her mother tripped and fell face down into the oregano. For a moment she lay there motionless, before rolling over onto her back, giggling and thrashing her arms and legs in the air like an upturned beetle.

Drink to me only with thine eyes,
And I will pledge with mine.
That thirst that from the soul doth rise, doth ask a drink divine.
But might I of Jove's nectar sup, I would not change for thine.

She finished the song, then hauled herself up onto her feet and brushed down her clothes.

Alice breathed an exaggerated sigh of relief, then turned her attention to the wooden trunk, which she dragged across the floor and into the swathe of sunlight cutting through the window. Throwing open the lid, she snatched up the photograph of Jane Dalotz and held it to her breast. Alice's heart pounded, her pulse raced, as she and the desecrated image of the young girl clung to each other like castaways on a raft, two lovers adrift in uncharted seas.

After a minute or so, Alice detached herself from the photograph and propped the image up against a wall. Then, with a reverence reserved only for the possessions of the dead, she began unpacking the rest of the trunk. She laid each item out on the floor: the purple velvet dress with the lace collar, the string of jet beads, the much-loved storybook *The Doctor and the Secret Room*, and the letter tied up in a blue ribbon.

With the shrine spread out before her, Alice again picked up the photograph, this time holding it at arm's length, thereby resisting the strange power it held over her. Alice studied Jane's face; the girl was turning away from the camera, head slightly bowed, though her seductive eyes looked directly into the lens, flirting with it, or perhaps with the man standing behind it. Or perhaps … Alice's heart pounded again … or perhaps Jane's sensual gaze was for her. Alice turned the photograph over and read the label on the back: "Jane Dalotz, photographed by Lewis Carroll."

Alice once asked her mother about Jane Dalotz. It was the day she first discovered the attic. Alice remembered it was a bitterly cold February night, a storm had blown in from the North, and the house and garden were covered with a blanket of snow. Alice had been sitting near the fire, threading her embroidery hoop, when she related to her mother the events of the day. How she found the attic, the trunk, and the photograph of Jane; and how Jane's lips had been cut away from the picture. But when Alice asked the question, "Who Was Jane Dalotz?" her mother only sighed, gazed up at the cracks in the ceiling, and replied, "Oh Alice, that's a very sad story. Ask your father about it when he returns from his travels. He knows more about it than I do."

But Alice's father hardly ever returned from his travels. He was a diplomat. Alice wasn't quite sure what a diplomat was, only that it meant her father was abroad for 10 months of the year. She would receive letters from him, postmarked Bombay, or Cairo, or Katmandu. Then once a year, at the beginning of December, Alice and her mother shivered on the platform of the local railway station, waiting for his train to arrive. The procedure was reversed at the end of January when they shivered and waved him off on his travels again.

The day after Alice's mother avoided answering the question about Jane Dalotz, Alice decided to ask the cook, the rosy-cheeked old woman, whose breasts swelled to twice their normal size during her regular bouts of laughter. She had been working at the house since long before Alice and her parents moved in. She was a part of its structure, foundations, walls, and roof. As settled as the clusters of swallows' nests clinging to the eaves, long after the fledglings upped and flew south for the winter.

The cook was dicing an onion to make soup. Alice climbed onto the stool next to her and asked the question outright … "Who was Jane Dalotz?"

"Ah! Now there's a story." Cook laid her knife aside. "That was before you moved here. Mrs. Dalotz was a wonderful woman, very grand, married to an army officer. Jane was their only child. She was as happy and as healthy as a child could be, until one day, while Jane was playing in the garden, she was bitten on the lip by a snake. The doctor was called in, but he couldn't do anything for her. She just withered away, the poor little lamb. Her mother sat with her during those long, painful days that followed. Mrs. Dodgson, a friend of the family, visiting at the time, sat with her through the long sleepless nights. But Jane's life just seemed to drain away from her, and some people say … "

Alice was never to hear what some people say, as the cook's story was cut short by Alice's mother coming in from the garden, carrying a basket of freshly harvested vegetables.

"Beatrice!" Alice's mother snapped. "Now don't go filling the girl's head with rumors and nonsense. Take no notice of her Alice."

And that was the end of it.

When Alice's father did return home from his travels that following winter, Alice tried several times to ask the question, "Who was Jane Dalotz?" but every time she broached the subject, a blustery wind passed through the house, and the chill of it left Alice speechless, her lips frozen in a petrified silence. The name of Jane Dalotz was never spoken of in the house again.

Following closely the rules of the ritual, Alice stretched her hands over the shrine laid out on the attic floor. Her fingers twitched nervously, as she picked up the letter, untied the blue ribbon, and then slid the single sheet of paper out of the envelope. The letter was addressed to Jane Dalotz and was signed by her father, Captain Andrew Dalotz.

"My dearest Jane,

"My heart is saddened by the news that reaches me. Every night I pray that you will recover from this terrible thing that has happened to you. Your mother and my dear friend, Lewis Carroll, have both written to me of your nightmares and visitations from demons. Your mother tells me that you writhe in agony, while she and the doctor stand by, helplessly watching over you … "

As always, when Alice read the letter, she wept over the tragic death of the young girl, the girl she had never met, and *would* never meet. She also wept for herself, cursing the wicked twist of fate that had trapped her in this dark place, alone with her secret morbid desires.

When the daily ritual was completed, Alice was struck by an idea. Leaping to her feet, she kicked off her shoes and tore at her clothes, until she stood naked before the shrine. Then she picked up Jane's plum-colored dress, slipped it over her head, and smoothed it down around her body. It fitted perfectly. Alice closed her eyes, lifted her arms to the skies, and danced a trance-like ballerina dance, finally collapsing to the floor, breathless and dizzy from the pirouettes.

When the room stopped spinning, Alice opened the storybook, *The Doctor and the Secret Room*, and began reading it out loud, "Once upon a time, there was a good and kind doctor." At the point where Dr. Caxton goes up into the attic and opens the door to his secret room, Alice fell silent. Out the corner of her eye, she glanced a movement, and she turned to see a door opening in the wall.

With slow, even steps she walked through the doorway and into the room beyond. She expected to see Dr. Caxton's strange medicines for colds, and flu, and gout, but what she found there was very different. The room was lit by black candles, the flickering flames casting ungodly shadows over the walls, where hung a single row of framed photographs. On a table at the far end of the room, someone had placed a bowl of cherries, and next to it a sign that read EAT ME.

Like a general inspecting his troops, Alice paraded past the gallery of captured images on the wall, stopping to examine each of them in turn. The photographs were all of young girls, each of them wearing Jane's velvet dress, and, most disturbing of all, each of them with their lips neatly cut away from their faces. Beneath the pictures hung brass plaques, reading: Alice Lidell, photographed by Lewis Carroll, Margaret Hatch, Charlotte Webster, Amy Hughes,

Florence Terry, all photographed in the studio of the ubiquitous Lewis Carroll.

After studying the photographs, Alice focused her attention on the bowl of cherries and the intriguing sign: EAT ME. She picked the largest cherry from the bowl, examined it for bruises, and when satisfied that it was clean, she popped it into her mouth. For a while she rolled it around aimlessly on her tongue, then when she finally bit into its smooth, shiny skin, something unexpected happened; instead of the familiar tang of cherry, her mouth filled with the foul, coppery taste of blood. Alice gagged and spat out the fruit. It was then that she heard the voice ... "Eat Me. Eat Me."

About three feet in front of Alice's face, a pair of moist lips hovered in the air, parting slightly to repeat the words over and over again. Then more lips appeared, until the walls of the room bowed outwards, bursting at the seams with a chorus of voices ... 'Eat Me. Eat Me.'

Alice closed her eyes and covered her ears, but unable to escape the rising crescendo of voices, she ran from the room, stumbling down the stairs, through the kitchen and out into the garden. Her heart pounded as she ran past her mother, asleep on a bench cradling an empty bottle of whiskey, down a path dissecting the vegetable garden, through a gap in a fence, and into the wild woods beyond. All the time the voices grew fainter, the further she distanced herself from the house ... "Eat Me. Eat Me."

On and on she ran, through thickets of brambles, skidding on silky patches of ferns, and leaping over shallow streams, until the voices were left far behind. Taking refuge under the branches of a hazel tree, she listened hard, but all she could hear now was the singing of birds and the occasional rustle of a small animal scampering through the undergrowth. She sat down and leaned against the tree. As she stretched out her arms, her hand touched something cold. There it was, lying in the grass next to her, the photograph of Jane Dalotz, the only love she had ever known.

Alice picked up the picture, her eyes brimming with tears. Whatever demons she had unleashed back there in the attic, the purpose of it all was now clear to her, for Jane's lips had been restored to the photograph. Lips so seductive that even the snake could not resist taking that one fatal poisonous bite. Never again would Alice have to ask the question, "Who Was Jane Dalotz" because she now held the answer in her hand. Quite simply, Jane Dalotz was the most beautiful person who ever lived.

As the warm tears trickled down Alice's face, she sensed that familiar magnetic pull from the photograph, and she leaned forward to kiss the lips of her lover. As her lips grazed the cold glass, she felt a tongue pressing into her mouth, and her own tongue responding to the warm embrace. And then she felt the bite, a sharp pain in her lower lip. She tried to pull away, but the picture melted into the contours of her face, then wrapped itself around her head and clamped tightly shut. She struggled for breath, but instead of the sweet, woodland air, her mouth filled with the bitter taste of sour cherries. Her fingers tore at the frame, as she tried to release herself from its iron grip. But it was no use. Alice's young body shuddered one last time, and then she drifted away, to the magical world, to the place where all of her questions would be answered.

———————

Two weeks after the funeral, an old man stood at the foot of Alice's empty grave. Gifted with everlasting life and free from her fear of death, she had moved on and was following a white rabbit that would lead her to a wondrous land. In the old man's hand was a copy of *The Doctor and the Secret*

Room, which he began to read out loud, "*Once upon a time, there was a good and kind doctor.*" When he finished reading, he closed the book and listened. Somewhere in the distance, Alice's mother was singing:

> *Drink to me only, with thine eyes,*
> *And I will pledge with mine.*
> *The thirst that from the soul doth rise, doth ask a drink divine.*
> *But might I of Jove's nectar sup, I would not change for thine ...*

The old man waited until the song ended, then pulled a brown paper bag from his pocket, took out a bright red cherry and popped it into his mouth. As he savored Alice's warm blood, Lewis Carroll reverted to his familiar shape and form, then slithered away down the path and disappeared into the bushes.

THIRTEEN

BACK AT THE VAMP-ART CAFÉ

Dr. Crispin Goswell finished his story to polite, though muted, applause. He sensed an atmosphere in the room. Brahmarāk Şhasa, an Indian vampire from Rajasthan, voiced the concern of many of those present. "I like this story, but I found it disturbing. I worry it may cause people to think that vampires drink blood. As you all know, we don't drink blood. In Bram Stoker's scurrilous fiction, Count Dracula exists by drinking blood from unwilling victims. Yet, in this story, we have the author of children's books savoring the blood inside a cherry. I'm not sure what this story means. Is Jane Dalotz a vampire, or is Lewis Carroll a vampire, or both? I'm aware of Lewis Carroll's photographs of young girls and the speculation about his intentions. He may or may not have had an unhealthy interest in his models. I did not, however, know that he was a shape-shifting vampire. Is it possible that he is the snake mentioned in the first vampire story ever told? The snake that tempted Adam and Eve?"

Dr. Goswell shrugged his shoulders. "I understand the point you're making, but not all stories are neatly packaged. Some have loose ends, while others inspire thought and debate. My interpretation of this story is this: I think the girls in the photographs have all been smitten and bitten by writer Lewis Carroll. My belief is when he photographed them, he drained them of their 'fear of death' and gifted them with everlasting life. I believe that both Jane Dalotz and Lewis Carroll are vampires and that Alice was chosen. Nowhere in the story does it say that vampires drink blood to survive. As we all know, the reason we bite is to release the tension caused by the 'fear of death.' And why do we do that? Because the 'fear of death' weighs heavily on this world, for animals, vegetables, and minerals. It pollutes the air we breathe. The human race is consumed by it and pursues nonsensical theories of an afterlife or reincarnation. They fight wars over whose theory is right. They are destroying this beautiful planet. Animals, vegetables and minerals all harbor a 'fear of death.' A Louis XIV récamier couch may fear that one day it will be destroyed and replaced. A tree fears that it will be used as firewood or fall and rot in the forest. It is a noxious gas that pours continuously from mortals. Our task as vampires, as angels of Ra, the orange spong, is to pick worthy subjects or objects, pierce their surface, drain away the poisonous 'fear of death' and stem its flow into the atmosphere. As vampires, our fangs are acupuncture needles. We are global acupuncturists, healing the planet, ridding it of putrefaction."

The vampires in the Vamp-Art Café fell silent for a full minute. Bubbles of thought burst like blood-filled blisters in the air. Dario Brone broke the silence. "I will leave you all to your private thoughts on Dr. Goswell's story. Perhaps we could discuss it at another time. It's getting late. Brahmarāk Şhasa mentioned the serpent in the first vampire story ever told and that brings us to the end of our storytelling for the evening. We will now finish with a solemn prayer and our final story that I will read myself. I ask you all to stand, bow your heads and join me in a prayer to Ra, the orange spong, taken from the wall of the Egyptian tomb of Shepenmut, the priestess of Thebes. After we have prayed, I will read *In the Beginning*, the first story from the Vampire Book of the Dead."

O orange spong

You God of Life, you Lord of Love,
All men live when you shine.

You are the crowned King of the Gods.
The goddess ISIS embraces you,
and enfolds you in all seasons.
Those who follow you sing to you with joy,
and they bow down their foreheads to the Earth
In gratitude for your radiant blessings.

O orange spong, You the King of Truth, the Lord of Eternity,
The Prince of Everlastingness,
You Sovereign of all Gods,
You God of Life, you Creator of Eternity,
You Maker of Heaven.
All the Gods rejoice at your rising.

O orange spong, You giver of all life,
The Earth rejoices when it sees your golden rays
People who have been long dead
come forward with cries of joy
to behold your beauties every day.
You go forth each day over Heaven and Earth.

O orange spong God of Life, you Lord of Love,
All men live when you shine.

FOURTEEN

IN THE BEGINNING

As Told by Dario Brone

Mortal men tell their version of the beginning, but they are blind and do not see. Hidden from mortals is the truth, a truth they will never comprehend. In a universe where nothing makes sense, everything is a mystery.

The Cosmos consists of galaxies of spongs floating in space like soap bubbles. Spongs are galactic orbs reflected in mirrors, seen through microscopes, telescopes, or viewed through kaleidoscopes. Spongs are sometimes invisible.

Before the re-birth of the Earth star, most of the universe was light, though there were areas of darkness where danger lurks. In one forgotten corner of the universe, the Earth star was dying. Left to rot by the occupants. It was a black hole in space where gravity was so strong, light could not escape. Yet there was still hope for the Earth star. This dying orb remained buoyant, lifted, and carried along on the fluttering wings of hawks. The hawks of Kubla Khan.

Kubla Kahn and his hawks existed before the beginning of time and will live until after the end of it. This Emperor of China lives outside of time and space in a spong of his own. He is the creator of spongs. In the darkness, Khan summoned Xanadu, one of his favorite hawks. He couldn't see the bird of prey in the darkness, but he heard and felt the beating of its wings, and felt his claws tearing into the leather cuff he wore on his wrist. Khan fumbled blindly in the darkness, found a door in the bird's chest, and opened it. Nestled inside was Ra, a beating heart, a glowing orb, a God, an orange spong. The orange spong throb, throb, a-throbbed.

The Emperor of China reached into the hawk's chest, grasped the orange spong, then tossed it several miles into the darkness. Moments later, Ra peeked over the skyline, shooting beams of orange light onto a barren terrain. It was the first new dawn in Earth star's Garden of Eden. As the desolate landscape revealed itself, Ra, the orange spong, summoned a flotilla of dark cloud ships with black sails, steered by cosmic energies and electrical sparks. The cloud ships rained down thunder, lightning, and torrents of rain. After seven days, the rain created four rivers: Pishon in the land of Havilah, Gihon in the land of Cush, the Tigris east of Assyria and the Euphrates. And from this newly watered earth grew plants: wheat, hazelnut trees, cucumbers, chrysanthemums, and cactuses. Then Ra, the orange spong, created animals, insects and birds: wasps, polar bears, meerkats, monkeys, parakeets, and the human race. Then Ra, the orange spong, created inanimate objects, gave them souls and gifted them with eternal life: chairs, lamps, shoes, and timepieces. Lastly, Ra, the orange spong, looked at the mountains, the soil, the sand, and the sea and gifted them all with immortality. Then, after his work was done, Ra, the orange spong, named everything in the Garden of Eden, "VAMPIRE."

In this new world, nothing died or withered. There was no sickness, no unhappiness, nothing was destroyed, killed, or eaten. And because death did not exist, nobody feared it. Nobody dwelt on mortality, or lived their life knowing it would end. There were no theories, philosophies, or religions to ponder the subject of the "meaning of life" because life went on forever. Nothing divided the inhabitants of the Garden of Eden, so there were no wars, hatred, or bigotry. The vampire tiger lived happily with the vampire windmill, and the vampire windmill lived happily with the vampire goldfish because everything in the Garden of Eden has a soul. A purpose. All things are equal. Everything is a jigsaw piece in a completed puzzle.

The Garden of Eden was Paradise.

Then Ra, the orange spong, looked down upon the Garden of Eden and throb, throb, a-throbbed its orange glow. "I have built this Paradise for all of you to enjoy forever, a place of balance and harmony. Vampires do not kill or eat other vampires, so the inhabitants of the Garden of Eden gain sustenance from a steady diet of imagination, creativity, ideas, laughter, and inspiration. I ask only this. I have created one sacred tree, the Tree of Finality. This tree is not to be touched, only gazed upon. Its fruit is not to be eaten. If you disobey this one rule, then you will be banished from Paradise to Paradise Lost, a Mirror-World where you will be mortal, where everything dies."

After a while, Adam and Eve, two human vampires, strayed from the path of goodness. In the beginning, they heeded the warning of Ra, the orange spong, and shunned the Tree of Finality. They avoided it like it was a plague until they forgot about its very existence. Then one day, a serpent appeared and reminded them. This serpent slithered through a wormhole between Paradise and Paradise Lost.

Eve was alone in a meadow when the snake slithered up to her. She was not afraid, as there were many snakes in the Garden of Eden. They meant no harm. She had danced with rattlesnakes, slept with black mambas, and spoken at length with vipers. The snake asked Eve if she had ever eaten the fruit hanging from the Tree of Finality. Eve blushed. "No,

Ra, the orange spong, said that if we eat the fruit from the Tree of Finality, then we will become mortal and be banished from the Garden of Eden. We will be driven from Paradise to Paradise Lost."

The serpent laughed. "That's not true. You will not become mortal. Ra, the orange spong, is trying to control you with fear. Ra wants to take charge of your free will and destiny. The fruit from the Tree of Finality will set you free. Try the fruit, what harm can it do?"

Tempted by the serpent, Eve picked a piece of fruit from the Tree of Finality and bit into it. It was delicious. And so, in turn, Eve tempted Adam, who also ate the fruit.

When Ra, the orange spong, sensed the harmony of the Garden of Eden disrupted, a tidal wave of anger swept over the land. Even the moles and earthworms could feel it underground. Quails quaked. Zebras stampeded. Ostriches buried their heads in the sand.

"What have you done?" demanded Ra, "Have you eaten from the tree of which I commanded you not to eat?"

Adam hung his head in shame. "The serpent tricked us, and we ate."

To Eve, Ra, the orange spong, said, "I shall surely increase your sorrow and pain. And Adam will rule over you and everything in your life."

And to Adam, Ra, the orange spong, said, "Because you listened to Eve, and you ate from the forbidden tree, I banish both of you to Paradise Lost, where you will know hardship all the days of your life. And I shall place hatred between you and Eve, and between your seed and between her seed. With the sweat of your body, you will feast upon each other and feast on those around you. And you will return to the ground, for from dust you are, and to dust you will return."

Then Ra, the orange spong, drove Adam and Eve out of the Garden of Eden, to till the soil, be mortals, and die in

Paradise Lost. All was quiet and harmonious again in the Garden of Eden. Nobody ever again ate the fruit from the Tree of Finality. After more time passed, Ra, the orange spong, saw that Paradise Lost, the Mirror-World, was polluted and dying. The seas were full of plastic and garbage. The ice caps were melting. Animals became extinct. Paradise Lost was putrid with the "fear of death." Nobody there cared about the future because everything died. Nothing was permanent. Paradise Lost was dying from neglect. The "fear of death" consumed Paradise Lost, and those who lived there created religion to make sense of their mortality. Selfishness and greed caused them to not go quietly into death but to resist the inevitable. That "fear of death" led to wars, destruction, and pollution. It made the inhabitants of Paradise Lost oblivious to the ailing health of their own world.

So it was that Ra, the orange spong, took pity on Paradise Lost and sent two human vampires into the Mirror-World. He called them Michael and Gabrielle, archangels, magicians and healers. Their mission was to behave as mortals – though undead – to infiltrate Paradise Lost and seek out those worthy of eternal life. On those chosen, the vampire angels practiced global acupuncture with their fangs. With one bite, the vampire fangs drained the chosen ones of their "fear of death," thus releasing the built-up tension and saving Paradise Lost from pollution.

Michael and Gabrielle wandered Paradise Lost creating more vampires ... that begat vampires that begat vampires, that begat vampires, that begat vampires, that begat vampires, that begat vampires, that begat vampires, that begat vampires, that begat vampires, that begat vampires, that begat vampires, that begat vampires, that begat vampires ...

And Ra, the orange spong, saw that it was good.

FIFTEEN

BACK AT THE VAMP-ART CAFÉ

At midnight, the witching hour, the vampires spilled out of the Vamp-Art Café and onto the dimly lit Chicago streets. It was 1924 in Chicago's Towertown. The smell of danger filled the back alleyways as Al Capone's speakeasies opened for business, and gangsters in Dorris 6-80 touring cars carried Thompson submachine guns to bump off stool pigeons. In the empty café, the staff cleared away the tables. Oliver Cramfish, the manager of the Vamp-Art Cafe, folded the tablecloths and napkins neatly into a bag. He dropped them off at the 24-hour Chinese laundry on his way home. Then, in the morning, he picked up the laundered linen as Ra, the orange spong, rose up over Lake Michigan.

Cramfish was last to leave the cafe. Before closing the door, he turned off the lights and scanned the darkness. All was quiet. The walls breathed a sigh of relief, then slept soundly, until the Vamp-Art Café opened for storytelling again.

OTHER BOOKS BY
ST SUKIE DE LA CROIX

Chicago Whispers: The History of LGBT Chicago Before Stonewall

The Memoir of a Groucho Marxist: A Very British Fairy Tale

Gay Press, Gay Power – contributor

Out of the Underground: Homosexuals, the Radical Press, and the Rise and Fall of the Gay Liberation Front

St Sukie's Strange Garden of Woodland Creatures – with Roy Alton Wald

Tell Me About It – with Owen Keehnen

Tell Me About It 2 – with Owen Keehnen

"Who Was Jane Dalotz?" in The Kiss of Death: An anthology of vampire stories."

"The Dinner Party or All's Well That Ends Well" in Midsummer Night's Dreams, edited by M. Christian.

"Jane Austen Must Be Turning in Her Grave" in Guilty Pleasures, edited by M. Christian

"I Fuck the Dead" in Book of Dead Things edited by Tina L. Jens and Eric M. Cherry

"Private Dick" in Noirotica 3: Stolen Kisses edited by Thomas S. Roche